Granite Lake Wolves

Wolf Signs

Wolf Flight

Wolf Games

Wolf Tracks

Wolf Line

Wolf Nip

Takhini Wolves

Black Gold

Silver Mine

Diamond Dust

Moon Shine

Takhini Shifters

Copper King

Laird Wolf

A Lady's Heart

Wild Prince

A full list of Vivian's print titles is available on her website

www.vivianarend.com

PRAISE FOR VIVIAN AREND

"Vivian Arend does a wonderful job of building the atmosphere and the other characters in this story so that readers will be sucked into the world and looking forward to the rest of the books in the series."
~ *Library Journal*

"Steamy and sweet complete with a whole host of colourful side characters and enough sub-plots to get your teeth into. A fab read!"
~ *Scorching Book Reviews*

"There's a real chemistry between the characters, laced with humor and snappy dialogue and no shortage of steamy sex scenes to keep things lively. The result is an entertaining, spicy romance."
~ *Publishers Weekly*

Silver Mine is an outstanding story. The author creates a world that invites readers for the ride of their lives."
~ *Coffee Time Romance Reviews*

Arend offers constant action and thrills, and her characters are so captivating and nuanced that readers will have a hard time guessing who the villains really are.
~ *RT Book Reviews*

WOLF NIP

NORTHERN LIGHTS EDITION

VIVIAN AREND

Wolf Nip
Copyright © 2013 by Arend Publishing Inc.
ISBN: 9781989507834
Edited by Anne Scott
Cover Design by Croco Designs
Proofed by Sharon Muha

For Lauren Dane, who wrote the first wolves I fell in love with. I blame her for my wolfie addiction, as well as my genre-hopping tendencies as an author. <3

1

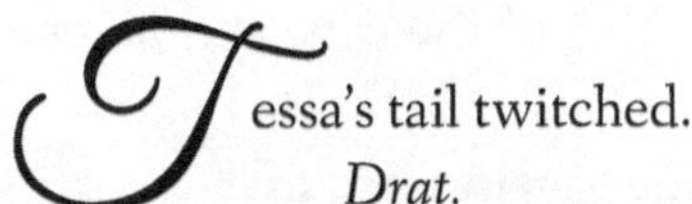

Tessa's tail twitched.

Drat.

She concentrated harder, crouching lower to the ground. Muscles steady, but ready to move in an instant. One deep breath followed after another as she attempted to calm her nerves. Every instinct screamed for her to squirm, to peek around. To check if all her parts were tucked out of sight.

But then it had been proven that some of her cat instincts were a trifle on the broken side.

In her cougar form, his scent wasn't strong enough to hit before his paw pads sounded, and by the time she heard him, there was no escape. A warm body slammed into her, and together they rolled from behind the barrier she'd chosen as a hiding spot. Before he could pin her in place, Tessa wiggled free and took off.

Fine, maybe he'd found her, but he hadn't won yet. She used her strong cat muscles to dash away through the maze of the gymnasium area.

No matter how fast she ran, though, her pursuer remained right on her tail. Literally on her tail, and when he playfully patted her hindquarters for the third time, Tessa gave up. She leapt for the narrow ledge along the wall where she'd shifted in the first place. Changing back to human and dressing only took a moment before she rejoined her big brother on the gym floor.

Tony had also shifted and pulled on nearly identical jeans and T-shirt to hers. His relaxed grin teased her from under his mop of blond hair. "I'd say you did better that time, but I'd be lying."

Tessa stuck out her tongue. "Someday I'll win."

"In your dreams. I am the king of the cats, and no one will take my crown."

She rolled her eyes and made gagging sounds.

Tony tweaked her nose. "Face it, brat, your skills lie in areas other than cat-and-mouse games."

And there was the opening she'd been waiting for. "Right. So in terms of my skills, did you remember I need your signature on that form at the bank?"

"Did you remember I said you were nuts?"

Tessa pulled her hair into a ponytail and resisted sticking out her tongue again. "You've said it so many times over the years, I figured it was code for *Hey, Sis, you rock.* You didn't see the place, Tony. It's incredible. Exactly the kind of establishment I want to manage. The setting is exquisite, and the area just screams eco-tourism, which you know as well as I do—"

"Stop. Not the eco-business thing." Tony covered his ears and groaned in mock pain.

Tessa pounced, grabbing hold of his forearms and dragging his hands free. "Eco-eco-eco-eco..."

They laughed together, and she knew everything would

be okay. She'd been trying since graduation to find a job that fit her skills. Seasickness had nixed the possibility of working for the family shifter-only cruise line, but her trip to the north had yielded one side benefit.

When she'd spotted the unique building tucked up against the trees, she'd nearly bounced into the ocean with excitement. She needed a little more cash to set her ideas in motion, and her brother had the credit rating to help her get established.

If he was willing to take the chance on her.

Tony guided them down the hallway toward the cafeteria. "I signed, sealed. Promised my firstborn kit. All those things. And yes, I'll admit the eco-tourism part was the selling feature. I'll back you on this one, Tessa, but please, if you need help, ask? You don't have to go it solo."

"I'm capable. Got the training, the experience. Heck, I graduated with higher marks than you did."

He shrugged. "You're a smart cookie, I'll give you that. But, girl, this is Alaska you're talking about. We've had a base in the area harbour for years with the cruise ships, but there aren't a lot of prides around. You're going to be the only cat in town."

She stopped dead in her tracks. "I don't know if I should give you a hug for being concerned or smack you across the head. Are you prejudiced, Tony? I would never have known, not with the way you've got friends in all the local wolf packs and—"

"That's not what I meant." Tony tugged her forward, and she went willingly enough, although confused how he would talk his way out of this one. "Shifters are cool, and I don't care what kind. But the reality is we go about things differently. You know that."

"Yeah. I shift into a cougar. My best friend Keri shifts

and, hey look, a wolf! Different, right? Next bit of kindergarten information you want to share with me, big bro? 'Cause this is so educational."

"Don't be a pain in the ass."

"Don't be a pain, period. What are you trying to say?"

Tony plopped into one of the plastic cafeteria chairs, and it groaned under his muscular weight. "Fine. Wolves. Pack. Alaska is filled with wolves who could be very territorial about a cat coming into their midst. You're good with people, Tessa, but wolves can be a tricky lot. Especially when they are *the* game in town."

She fluttered her fingers. "Pshaw. I met their chief pooh-bah. He's super nice. And Keri is mated to one of the Granite Lake pack, so I'm already a kissing cousin. There's not going to be trouble. Really. I promise not to go on any wild rampages and stir up trouble, no matter how tempting."

Tony raised a brow. "A town full of dogs, and you don't feel the slightest urge to cause mischief?"

All the crazy ideas that flashed to mind could be blamed on that faulty instinct she was working on fixing. "Of course not. I'm a grown woman. This is my career, and I'm capable of suppressing a few urges."

A crazy expression crossed his face, and Tessa slammed up a hand. Oh no, they were not going there.

"Don't. Don't even think about giving me advice regarding any other kinds of urges. I will not listen. I will not hear. You cease to exist...blah, blah, blah."

Tony sighed. "You're a cat."

"You're so annoying."

"They're wolves."

Tessa wadded up her napkin and threw it in his face.

"So, what have you got planned for the next year? Working three cruises? Going to take some time off in the fall and go exploring?"

Her brother stared at her so hard she swore she heard the gears in his brain grinding, but he was smart enough to drop the subject and switch to chatting about his future plans.

Because no matter how comfortable shifters were with sex, talking with her brother about mattress mamboing was on the list of things she really didn't want to do.

Besides, the point he'd planned on raising she'd already thought through. The place she wanted to buy was on the outskirts of Haines, and wolves were a well-established part of the northern community. Wolves, like all shifters, enjoyed their sexual escapades, but they were more territorial and possessive than the average cat, in bed and out of it.

Cats and bears and other shifters picked mates when the time was right. Wolves followed some mystical mumbo jumbo and fell in *twue wuv* when their animal sides sniffed the right person. Which—ick. Just ick.

Well, maybe not *ick*—she'd seen it work for her friend, but there was no way she wanted to settle down yet. She'd make sure any urges of the naughty sort were satisfied during playtime with humans. Or visitors to the area. Or battery-operated boyfriends—the list of possibilities was endless.

This stage of the adventure was about establishing a top-notch resort in the north. And sex, while always enjoyable, was a low priority. Tessa nodded to herself, pleased she'd gotten that straightened out.

She turned her attention back to her brother and tried

not to allow her fanciful daydreams about the new resort distract her.

~

MARK WEAVER STARED in dismay across the table at his boss. "But—"

"I'm sorry."

"I've only been here for two months."

The older man sighed. "Which means, according to the rules, now that the season is slowing down and I have to let staff go, you're the first on the release list."

Dammit. "I enjoyed this job. And I worked hard. And—"

"Mark, please don't make this any tougher than it already is." Mr. Remy pushed the pink slip closer. "You are a good worker, but I can only afford to keep two full-time staff over the winter."

Double dammit. Mark nodded. "I understand."

"If you need work in the spring, I'd be happy to hire you back on. And I wrote you up a letter of recommendation." A slim envelope joined his release papers on the tabletop. "If I can help you get a job, let me know."

Mark shook the man's hand and grabbed his things, escaping into the crisp fall sunshine of late August. Well, that was an unexpected and bitter twist. He hopped on his mountain bike and considered where he wanted to waste the rest of the gorgeous, yet annoying day.

Some tough, all-out physically draining exercise would help. If nothing else, it would make his body match the crappy mental state he was now in. Of all the blasted luck.

Instead of going home, he headed toward the opposite

side of town and the Granite Lake pack house. Maybe there would be a few other members hanging around he could convince to join him for a backcountry jaunt. Something to distract him from the fact he was once again unemployed, unattached and unhappy.

Life sucked. It really did.

It wasn't as if he wanted to point fingers and attach blame to make himself happier. He just had shitty luck. His education had never gotten him a job. The jobs he did find vanished from the work pool right under his feet. Okay, to be honest he had mucked up a couple times, but overall he was credited as a hard worker, a great guy...and still shown the door.

He wasn't going to be forced to sleep in the streets—the family legacy covered that one. Nope, a roof over his head wasn't an issue, although the house had become a bit of a trap. He couldn't leave Haines without losing his rent-free home. He couldn't sell it to use the funds to set up a place elsewhere. The red tape was frustrating as all get-out, and even that morning he'd gotten a reminder of the chaotic state of his housing affairs.

The nicely written proposal for him to sell his unique home to some eco-adventure B&B developer. An awesome idea if it weren't illegal, and thus impossible.

Not to mention, there was his Gramps to consider.

He had food on the table—he wasn't lazy, or too proud to work any kind of temporary job to keep the money coming in, but a real job? Something he could do for a career? Elusive as the northern lights on a summer day.

He propped his bike against the wall of the pack house and shuffled into the common room, the scent of fresh-baked brownies making his mouth water. Less than a dozen pack were gathered in the room, chilling out in easy chairs as they read, a couple of older members facing each other down over a chess board.

Missy, the pack Omega, swung into the room, her hands full of baking, and he rushed forward to help. "Not that I'm going to complain, but why are you cooking?"

She smiled and shook her blonde curls as he took the tray. "I promised Tad I'd stay at the pack house today, and if I'm here, I may as well be productive."

Mark carried the goodies around the room as he considered her words. That was one of the coolest parts of the Granite Lake pack—even the top levels of leadership were right there and involved. Missy and her mate Tad were occupied with their young family, busy with personal jobs and caring for pack in their weird and wonderful all-knowing-emotional-touchy-feely Omega wolf-shifter way, but they never stopped doing what needed to be done.

Of course, by the time he'd made the rounds and deposited the remaining goodies on the table, Missy was seated in a chair at the side of the room waiting for him.

Drat. He should have known he couldn't avoid a little heart-to-heart. He lowered himself into the chair beside her and wondered how long he could distract her from her lecture, or interrogation, or whatever it was she had planned. "Where are your kids?"

Missy shook a finger in his face. "Don't even try it, buster."

Mark snorted. So. That's how long. "Seriously, I'm curious."

"Forget my kids. Why are you at the pack house at this time of day, wearing that kind of face, young man?"

"You like this face better?" He cocked one eye shut and

grimaced. "Arghh, I've been given me walking papers. Off the plank and into the brig with me, matey."

"Oh, Mark. I'm sorry. I thought you were enjoying yourself at the factory." Missy leaned back in her chair, sympathy on her face.

"Low season approaches. You know how it goes. Don't worry, I'll be fine. I'll find a new job soon enough."

She nodded slowly. "You always do. That's not a problem. But..."

Mark took another bite of his brownie and waited. There was obviously something she wanted to share. He stared out the window and calculated the most difficult bike route he could attempt after this little discussion was done. Death-drop highway? His thighs would be screaming.

Screaming would be good.

A soft touch to his knee brought his attention back to Missy who watched him carefully.

He forced himself to focus. "What?"

"I asked if you'd ever thought about going into business for yourself?"

A jolt of adrenaline shot through him. Of all the things she could have said, that was on the least expected list. "Umm. No."

"Because you don't...what? Think you can do it? Don't want the responsibilities?"

"Of course not. I mean, I just had never thought of it." She'd managed to jerk all thoughts of gloom and doom from his mind and instead fill it with confusion. "Why would you suggest that?"

She shrugged. "Well, for as long as I've been around the pack, I've seen you handle many kinds of jobs. For different lengths of times, yes, but they all seem to have a common 'handy man' theme to them. So I was wondering why you've never set up a personal business and offered those same services under your own name."

Mark felt something hard hit his jaw and figured it had to be the floor.

Missy went on. "While you might have slow periods, you'd be able to make more money during the prime season than you do now working for someone else."

His mouth went dry.

"You'd have to deal with the legal and financial aspects, of course, but—"

Whatever else she was going to say was smothered under his arm as he leapt up, bounded over to her chair and enveloped her in a huge bear hug. "You're a genius."

When he released her, she patted his cheek. "So I've heard. I take it this means I helped?"

"Darn tooting you did." Ideas flashed into his brain. Probably not the same ones she would have figured on triggering, but that was fine. He was no longer looking for a way to burn off his pissy mood. Now he needed to get home and make some plans. "You mind if I run?"

She grinned. "Go. I'd never stand in the way of a man's progress."

He stopped beside his bike and rummaged through his pockets. He could have sworn he'd shoved the letter in there after he'd read it that morning.

His letter of recommendation. His firing papers. An old grocery list. Finally, the one he was looking for.

A very expensive envelope containing the letter that had made him laugh out loud over breakfast. The out-of-the-blue offer to buy his house. The potential buyer hadn't known about the clauses that made their plans impossible.

But if he made a few adjustments to the offer, maybe there would be a middle ground where they could meet. He couldn't sell out, but he could see his place as an awesome B&B location.

Mark Weaver, the habitually unemployed was ready to become Mark Weaver, chief resort-maintenance coordinator. And he wouldn't even have to leave his own home to do it.

2

———

A loose strand of hair flapped in front of her face until Tessa tucked it behind one ear. She stared at the approaching shoreline. She'd chosen to arrive via the ocean from Skagway over to Haines instead of driving the six hours from Whitehorse. Not only did it make the trip shorter, it gave her another glimpse of the spectacular house.

Even though the slow rise and fall of the water was muted on the ferry, she was hanging on to her stomach control by a thin thread. Motion sickness made it tough to linger on deck, but she wanted one more confirmation her idea was more than a wild fantasy.

She shoved a piece of gum into her mouth and chewed rapidly to distract herself. Nothing had been finalized, but she'd made a decision. She was determined to establish a B&B in Haines, somewhere. Her first choice of location was still number one on the list. Hopefully dealing with this Mark Weaver fellow in person would help smooth the roadblocks she'd hit.

His email response to her offer to buy his house had

been unexpected. It wasn't an outright *no*, which was positive, but she hadn't expected a *maybe* type answer. She knew better than to dismiss his counterproposal out of hand. The best business ideas usually went through a couple modifications before resolving into a working solution, so she'd packed her bags, taken the bulls by the horns, *yada yada yada*, and arranged a trip to settle the details one way or another.

The ferry rounded the point and the vista changed. Tessa grabbed the railing with both hands and leaned forward, eager to spot her target.

Here the northern portion of the Pacific Inside Passage opened into a wide bay, with the town of Haines spread over the center left section. The harbour sat as the base, houses and buildings rising in neat layers up the gentle mountainside. Traces of civilization poked through the trees lining the road as it meandered up the valley to the distant mountain pass. Drivers taking that route would eventually hit Haines Junction and the intersection that led back to Whitehorse or into the bulk of the Alaskan landmass.

Her goal sat farther to the east. The town continued to spread in a thin line along the narrow highway up to Chilkoot Lake, one of the destinations each fall for thousands of spawning salmon. The pretty river descending from the lake sparkled in the sunshine like a beacon. She glanced to the right of it, sighing as her target came into sight.

The enormous paddle wheeler sat crosswise to the waters of the bay. It should have looked out of place tucked into the trees, but it was as if the boat continued its journey up a river, the dense northern forest on either side passing slowly as the ship carried cargo and passengers toward remote destinations.

Tessa rested her chin in her hands and grinned. There was a full deck circling the second story, just like she'd remembered. It would be perfect for individual sitting areas for the cabins she would turn into high-class staterooms. The third story had a raised back section that would be her private living quarters, while the front contained the spectacular window-filled area that would be the feature room of the entire B&B.

She could picture it now—a long communal dining table on the right side, and easy chairs and cozy private seats gathered around the massive fireplace she would have built at the far end of the room.

There would be dorm and entertainment rooms on the lower levels, along with storage for all the outdoor play equipment people could want. Tessa caught herself bouncing on her heels as ideas flooded her brain.

This was going to be so awesome, she could hardly wait.

The paddle wheeler disappeared behind a bend in the coastline, and Tessa returned to her vehicle. Time to move forward with her plans, full steam ahead, and all that. She clicked her phone back on and flipped through messages as she waited for the ferry to dock and start unloading. *Tony, Tony, parents, old boyfriend, another guy. Another. Her brother. Another recent date.*

She erased all but the family messages without blinking. Guy friends were fun, but there was little use in keeping touch with any males back home. Haines was going to be her new hunting grounds, although she'd be careful not to use that terminology with anyone who didn't know, and love, cat-shifter wit.

Keil Lynus. There was a name she'd been hoping to see. She put through a return call and waited, tapping her manicured fingers on the wheel as the tone sounded.

"Keil here."

"Tessa Williams. We met back in July, I'm Keri Smith's friend."

He chuckled. "I remember. How have things been since you dry-docked yourself?"

Nice. The Alpha of the Granite Lake pack had a sense of humour. "Sold the private sailboat and abandoned my bucket-list plans to sail around the world solo."

"Sounds like a good idea. What can I help you with?"

Tessa started her engine and followed the line of cars exiting the ferry. "Two things. One, you're a wolf and all, and I'm a cat, but I thought it would be polite to let you know I'm moving into town."

There was a short pause before he responded. "Not a problem. Granite Lake is fairly progressive. I'm pretty sure you won't have any issues with pack bothering you. If anyone gives you grief, call me and I'll deal with it."

The low rumbly sound of his voice made shivers run up and down her spine. Gad, too bad the man was taken already. He was like this huge mass of sexy shifter, but she knew better than to mess with a mated wolf. She drew a solid black line through his name with her mental marker and got back to business. "I knew I could trust you. I told my brother that."

"Is he moving here as well?"

Was that concern she heard? More than one feline entering the picture changed things? "Oh, no. Tony just thought me being the only cat around might cause concerns...or am I wrong? Is there a pride in Haines I don't know about?"

Keil laughed. "I think Haines is too transient a community for a pride to settle in. We get the occasional puma, lynx or cougar staying for the summer season, but if you consider that many part-time jobs in the area involve water..."

"Ick." He was right, that would be an issue for most cats. She turned down the road leading to the paddle wheeler and took her car up to just over the limit. "Okay, no pride. That's fine, I make friends easily."

"I'm sure you do." Yes, he was amused now. Tessa ignored it. Wolves took themselves far too seriously at times. "Was there something else?"

On to the more important topics. "You run Maximum Exposure, right? Adventure trips, hikes, stuff like that?"

"I do. We don't have anything lined up in the next couple weeks except a glacier trip, but if you're interested—"

Tessa laughed and cut in as quickly as possible. "Wait, not for me. At least, not right now. I'm asking because I have a business proposition. I'm planning on setting up a B&B and want to offer excursions to the visitors. Instead of hiring my own guide and stealing bookings from you, is there a way for us to work together?"

He didn't answer immediately, but when he did the touch of an adult humouring a child had vanished. "That's very thoughtful of you to offer. I'd need to sit down with you in a more formal setting to find out what you're considering, but it could be a great help for both of us."

Gotcha. One of her biggest concerns and she could already see it being settled. "My father always says not to reinvent the wheel. Maximum Exposure has a sterling reputation. I would love to meet with you at your convenience."

"I'll check my calendar. Is there an address I can email you at? I'll send along a list of information I'll need to know."

She gave him her contacts, slowing to stare at the house that was now across the road from her. "I doubt I'll be ready until the spring, so there's no huge rush, but I look forward to hearing from you."

Keil hung up and Tessa concentrated on finding a place to park her car. Another item to add to her to-do list. Parking for the B&B—because right now there was only space for two cars, and she was really, *really* close to the bumper of the vehicle in front of her.

She slipped out, eager to look over her surroundings.

MARK JOTTED DOWN a few more numbers, the table he'd commandeered littered with notes. When the eco-developer showed up tomorrow, he'd be prepared to wow them with the plan. So ready, they couldn't ignore the beauty of the proposal.

Oh Lordy, let them see how brilliant this idea could be. While the alternative was setting up a handyman service, working at home would be better for so many reasons.

A long, low whistle sounded from the front of the room. Mark glanced up to see his grandfather staring out the window, both hands pressed against the glass as he peered intently toward the road.

"What's up, Gramps?"

"There's someone on your bumper. Another lost tourist, I bet. I'll go give them directions." Grandpa Josiah dragged his hands through his hair before patting down his shirt. He shuffled toward the stairwell.

That was too weird. Mark rose from his chair and paced across to the old man's side. "What do you mean you'll go give directions? Isn't this when you suggest I go downstairs and... Holy cow."

Okay, now he knew why his grampa was willing to tackle the stairs. The most gorgeous woman he'd ever seen stood beside his car, her long blonde hair waving in the breeze. She wore a brilliant blue sweater that emphasized every curve, fitted pants that highlighted the swells of her hips when she turned toward the water.

He would have pressed his face against the glass for a better look, but his grampa was there. Instead, Mark pretended nonchalance. "You're right, must be a lost tourist. I'll take care of her."

"See if she wants to stay until supper. I like company." Gramps had returned to the window.

"I thought you were going back to the pack house to eat."

Gramps grinned. "If she's staying, so am I."

Mark laughed. "Casanova. Be nice, old man."

His grampa waved a hand briefly. "Ah, you know I'm kidding. Nothing like a bit of lovely scenery to brighten a man's day, though. Go on, help the greenhorn."

Mark took the stairs by twos, puffing slightly by the time he'd reached the bottom level and the main entrance to the unusual house. He paused for a moment and peeked in the mirror beside the door, tidying his hair. Because, well, even if all he was doing was providing directions, no use in scaring her off.

He slipped outside, the freshness of the fall rushing around him.

Home. The only home he'd ever known. The northern seasons were familiar and well loved, including winter. The upcoming cold days and long nights didn't scare him. Not if he knew his Gramps was happy, and there was food on the table.

He was a simple man with simple needs, really.

It took a moment to spot his mystery woman. She wasn't where he'd expected. For some reason she'd crawled on top of her car hood and was up on her tiptoes examining his house.

Mark had never had a peeping tom like this one. He stepped across the lawn space. "Hello. Can I help you?"

She landed on her heels, her brilliant smile dazzling him. Bright green eyes snapped to meet his and somewhere deep inside his wolf rumbled awake.

"Are you Mark Weaver?"

"I am."

She clasped her hands together and bounced, literally, setting the entire car into motion. "Awesome. I'm Tessa, and I'm so glad to meet you."

Tessa. The name didn't register, but he automatically accepted her outstretched hand intent on helping her down off the hood.

Only instinct kept him vertical as she jumped lightly and landed beside him. The rest of him was a bundle of unplanned reactions, his wolf lurching to the surface and damn near howling in delight. The wind caught her hair again, ruffling it around her face. The breeze also brought her scent to him, and his mouth watered.

His body grew tight with need. His legs quivered.

"Ahem."

Mark jerked to attention. Tessa stood in front of him, her fingers caught in his, their bodies nearly touching. Sometime in the past ten seconds, he'd lowered his head toward her neck and taken a good long sniff.

It was like shooting a bottle of moonshine except the

hangover kick arrived simultaneously with the pleasure buzz.

"Mark, if you don't mind, I need my hand back." She grasped him around the wrist and tugged herself free from his clasp.

Embarrassed and yet excited at the same time, Mark let her go and forced himself to stand in place rather than crowd forward. There had to be a protocol he wasn't aware of that explained how you were supposed to react upon meeting your mate for the first time.

Mate. Yeah, his once-and-forever, fated-and-soon-to-be-mated woman. Once he found out a few minor details, like who she was, they could get down to the important stuff. Like him carrying her inside, finding a bed.

She tucked her hair behind her ear and batted her lashes, and his heart raced. *Patience, Mark. Patience...*

"Tessa. What brings you to Haines?"

"I'm here—"

He meant to give her time to answer. Meant to ask her in. Meant to do all sorts of things, actually, but what he did was lose control. He closed the distance between them, cupped his hand around the back of her neck and dragged them together so he could kiss her.

Whatever she planned on telling him was lost as his lips covered hers.

The taste of her? Ambrosia. The feel of her against his body? He'd died and gone to heaven. She nestled in tighter and her breasts rubbed his chest. His wolf nudged him harder, and he was powerless to resist the command, tangling their tongues until air became a dire need.

But the idea of stopping was unthinkable.

His wolf wanted more. Forget making it into the house and a bedroom, the beast wanted him to pick her up and wrap her legs around his waist. Lean her back over the car hood and take her right there. Strip her down and wallow in her scent and sex it up until they were both too sated to move.

Mark's human side figured most of that was dandy as well. He was far enough gone in lust that even the sex-in-public bit didn't sound like *too* bad of an idea.

Two cool hands cupped his burning-hot cheeks as Tessa managed to disengage their lips and wiggle away until her face returned to view. She was smiling, but confusion clouded her pretty eyes. "Hi. I think we should start this again. I'm Tessa Williams. I sent you a proposal to buy your house."

Shock was a good mood killer. Icy-cold restraint returned. "You're T. Williams?"

She wiggled out of his clutches and straightened her sweater. "I am. It's a beautiful place. We'll need to make a few changes though. If you don't mind me looking around, I'm sure we'll be able to come to an agreement."

Mark pulled his mouth shut. *This* was the person who wanted to purchase his home? "You're not supposed to be here until tomorrow."

"I was too eager to see the place to hang out in Whitehorse overnight. We can wait until the scheduled time for the meeting if that's better for you." Tessa pulled out a small mirror and lipstick, and touched up her lips with a fiery red colour he was tempted to lean over and lick off. He battled his wolf into submission.

Stubborn beast didn't want to talk. *Want to take.*

Mark got the sentiment, but... "We can discuss the house in a minute. First..."

His wolf poked him again, and this time he wasn't too distracted by lust to get the message. He took another breath, running his gaze over her entire body. Analyzing the way she stood, the way she'd moved.

Tessa crossed her arms in front of her, which only framed those flawless breasts a little more. "Yes?"

"I'm a wolf."

She nodded slowly. "I figured that out about two seconds after we met. And this is important...why?"

"You're a cat."

A cute pout appeared on her succulent lips. "You have issues with that?"

Mark shook his head even as he wondered how in the world this was going to work out. "You're perfect."

Light laughter escaped her. "Thank you, but I'm not sure what brought that on."

Good grief. If she'd been a wolf, he wouldn't need to have this conversation. They would have met and known they were the one for each other. As it was, his wolf continued to do the lupine equivalent of pacing, and it was a pretty damn uncomfortable sensation.

There must be more logical ways to approach this, but his logic meter had gone out of whack at the first sniff. The words blurted from him like homing missiles.

"My wolf says you're my mate."

Tessa's eyes widened. "Oh, really?"

He nodded. "That's why I kind of attacked you back there. The kiss and all."

"Okay, I wondered about that." Tessa glanced him over then shrugged. "Well, that's interesting. So, do you want to meet regarding my proposal now, or tomorrow?"

Confusion swirled with need, making his brain foggy. *"That's interesting?* That's all you've got to say about me telling you we're mates?"

She raised a brow. "No, *your wolf* said we're mates. My

cat says you're kinda cute, but we don't do mates like you guys. We're not into the insta-just-add-water thing."

He was going to fall over. "You're saying you don't want to be my mate?"

"Are you saying you love me?" she snapped back. "As in, you know all about me. What my hopes and dreams are. What makes me smile and what makes me cry and you want to spend the rest of our lives together because I complete you?"

Mark stuttered to a stop. "Well, no. But that will come. It always does, for wolves."

Tessa stepped closer and laid her hand on his arm. "But I'm not a wolf. I want to be in love before I mate anyone. That's important to me. We make a choice, our humans and our animal sides. I'm not trying to be cruel, but I'm sorry. We're not mates. Not yet."

3

———

She felt horrid. A terrible big bully who had taken away a child's favourite toy. Seeing Mark's face fall as she pulled back was like watching the rain clouds roll in and soak a picnic.

But darn it all. This was important to her as well.

Mark rallied himself. Coughed a couple times. Took a deep breath, his nose wrinkling up immediately.

Oops, her scent. Double drat. "Better not do that around me for a bit," Tessa suggested.

He nodded, held out his arm. "If nothing else, let's move the discussion inside. We have a lot to talk about, and standing on the road isn't the most comfortable place. I can show you the house."

She caught hold of his elbow. Her hand curled around his biceps and she had to smile. Nice muscles hidden under the flannel. Broad shoulders. That dark head of hair just screamed "run your fingers through me and mess me up". Perfect length as well that when she made fists, there'd be something to grab hold of.

And those eyes? Darkest of dark chocolate with a lovely hint of...golden flecks?...in the irises.

"Ahem."

It was her turn to realize she'd been staring at him and not moving anywhere. "Just checking you out."

Mark snorted. "You certainly are honest. Like what you see?"

"Oh, definitely." Of all the guys who could've popped out of the woodwork and announced they were mates, she wasn't going to argue with the exterior packaging on this one. She leaned up on tiptoe and brushed a loose strand of hair off his forehead.

His entire body shook as a shiver rolled through him. "Inside? Now, please?"

"Sure." She matched their paces, allowing him to lead up the walkway. All the while her brain took notes regarding improvements and changes to be done. The path would have to be widened, plus she'd add a few more flowerbeds on the left side. The exterior boards of the ship were well maintained, though, freshly painted that summer if she guessed right. "You've done a great job taking care of the place. The paddle wheeler looks as if it's in great shape."

"To be honest, the outside is better than the inside. Basic repairs and slapping up new paint is easy. The inside? Well, you'll see in a minute." He swung open the door and Tessa zipped in eagerly.

A massive staircase stood before her, the huge expanse of steps branching off on either side of a landing visible just above head level. There were solid oak railings, wood trim on the walls, and elegant chandeliers sparkled overhead in the sun shining through the windows.

She clutched her hands together and bounced. It was

exactly what she'd hoped. This would be the main entrance. The guests could go from here—

A soft touch on both shoulders brought her feet back in contact with the floor. "You're scaring the dust bunnies."

"Sorry." Tessa turned to face him, letting her happiness show in her smile. "It looks gorgeous. What were you worried about inside?"

Mark pointed to the right, the passage reaching out into the darkness like the entrance to a secret catacomb. "Chaos in the corners. My family used the place for a variety of things, and each time they tore down and put up walls as they pleased. When I inherited, I gave up on the bottom two levels and concentrated on fixing the upstairs the way I wanted it."

"That's okay." It was brilliant, actually. "It's best to renovate based on current needs, anyway. May I look around?"

Mark gestured her forward. "Be my guest."

Tessa slipped past him, his *hmmm* of approval as their bodies rubbed together making her smile. Okay, she didn't know him yet, but the *getting to know* could be a lot of fun.

She peeked through door-frames and around posts. While the walls were in odd places, there wasn't a ton of trash stashed in piles, or extra boxes. He wasn't a pack rat, which was nice to know. All this room to spare, it would have been tempting for a person to fill it to the rafters with junk.

She came back and tugged him toward the stairs. "Chaos is right. Some of the walls aren't vertical. Are the support beams solid?"

"Structurally, she's as sound as when she was built in the 1910s. They dry-docked her in the 1950s."

Walking up the staircase made her heart beat faster. "It's like a trip on the Titanic."

Mark laughed. "I hope not."

"Oh, I meant the elegance. So *so* pretty." She ran her fingers over the thick wood trim, and happiness welled up. Tessa twirled on him. "Can we talk business?"

"Let's go up one more floor. I'll make us a drink. Then we can discuss your proposal."

She'd lost her ability to concentrate, so focused on what could be accomplished in the incredible place. "Sure. Sorry."

Mark caught her chin with his fingers. "Stop apologizing. This is no longer your typical business meeting."

His hand was warm and felt wonderful against her skin. "Does that expression you're wearing mean you plan to kiss me again?"

He straightened slightly, caught in the middle of bending in closer—probably to kiss her. "There you go again with the blunt talk."

"I don't mind kissing," Tessa admitted. "Only I think we should figure out the other details of the arrangement first."

"And then we can get back to the kissing? Deal." He grinned, his teeth flashing white. "Oh, and heads up. My grampa is upstairs waiting to meet you."

Well now. "That was quick. What did you do, teleport him in while I was exploring?"

Mark guided them upward, the long risers of the stairs passing underfoot as he held her arm. "He spent the night. He's got a place in the seniors' lodge, but he loves coming over when he can. It's because of him..."

His voice faded and her curiosity tweaked. Before she could ask him more, though, distraction in the form of incredible shiny things burst into view. "Oh, Mark. It's lovely."

The top of the third flight of stairs opened onto a large, circular room, with aged hardwood underfoot, and gold fixtures. Behind the enormous windows of the upper level of the paddle wheeler, the spread of Haines Bay was revealed, sun shimmering off the water like millions of diamonds.

All her plans would fit perfectly in the space. The dining hall would go here. She spun and grinned harder as she spotted a wood-burning fireplace already settled against the north wall, comfortable chairs gathered around it. A passage led toward the back where she imagined the bedrooms and bath were hidden.

Even the kitchen was like she'd envisioned it, with brass instead of gold in the finishing touches. Industrial-sized ovens, two of them, were mounted on the wall, along with a double-sized fridge and a stovetop that had enough burners she imagined they could cook dinner for a couple dozen without batting an eye.

She rested her elbows on the enormous island and stared around her happily. It. Was. Perfect.

Her gaze fell on Mark, and his expression made her pause. "What?"

"You don't even know you're doing it, do you?"

"Doing what?" Tessa straightened and joined him. Adjusted his collar. Brushed a spot of dust off his elbow. Turned to look out—

She was jerked to a stop as Mark snagged her around one wrist. He kept a firm grip as he led her toward the comfortable chairs by the fireplace. "You took off like a whirling dervish. I think you set new land-speed records as you raced around the place."

"I love the house." He'd said not to apologize anymore, so she wouldn't, focusing instead on how incredible the place was. "You've done a wonderful job up here."

"Thanks. The kitchen was my parents' fault. They're both gourmet chefs, and that was their idea of basic necessities."

Oh, nice. Another point in his favour. "Does that mean you can cook?"

Mark nodded. "Fairly well."

"Don't you let him tell you lies, young lady." An elderly gentleman emerged from a door down the hall. He paced toward them, his grey and white hair contrasting with the leathery brown of his skin. "My grandson is a marvelous cook. Although I'm the one you want to call to man the barbecue."

She accepted his offered hand and shook it firmly. "Nice to meet you, sir. I'm Tessa Williams."

"My grandfather, Josiah." Mark fidgeted for a moment, the action strange on his big bulk. "I'll just...ahhh, put on the water for drinks."

He'd reached the point where he either had to run away and do something stupid like make tea, or Tessa would end up back in his arms. She'd made it clear their situation wasn't going to proceed as normal.

Damn. Drat. Shit.

Mark opened the freezer but resisted sticking his head inside, instead allowing the icy coldness to pour over his heated skin and provide a little relief.

His mate wanted nothing to do with him. Well, maybe that wasn't accurate. She'd kissed him back eagerly enough.

She'd been eyeing him with a rather pleased expression on her face, so there was hope, albeit smaller than he'd like.

At this moment he'd prefer them to be tucking themselves away in the master bedroom and checking out the springs on the mattress. Although, Gramps...

Gramps was a wolf. He'd understand.

But no, instead of answering the burning call igniting his every cell, he was farting around in the kitchen listening to the melodious sound of her voice as she chatted with Gramps.

Tessa laughed, and his body reacted.

He stared across the room and considered his options. She seemed serious about waiting. How on earth would he manage that when his wolf rustled hard enough to make him want to crawl out of his skin? Or out of his clothes and into his fur, if nothing else.

He grabbed his phone off the table where he had his work spread out, slipping toward the balcony door. "I'll be a minute. Gramps. If you want to show her the rest of the upstairs, go for it."

Mark didn't wait for them to respond, just shoved the French doors open and fled into the fresh air. Running away from the scent of her in the hopes he'd be able to find a little more control.

This couldn't be the first time someone had sniffed an unusual mate. He knew of at least one other in the pack. He punched in the familiar numbers and waited, one hand on the railing as he sucked in the refreshing air off the ocean.

"Yo. Heard the news you got sacked." TJ Lynus was another middle-of-the-packer in the Granite Lake wolves and an all-round good guy. "Want to drown your sorrows tonight? Pam's working the graveyard shift. I'm free to go carousing, so to speak."

With everything else on his mind, Mark had forgotten he'd been laid off. "That was days ago. It's old news, and I'm not upset or anything. I have something important to ask you, though. Regarding Pam."

"Really?" TJ's laid-back attitude vanished, even over the phone, becoming protective. "What do you need to know about my mate?"

How the heck did he ask this? Mark snorted. Maybe he needed to take a page from the straight-out honesty Tessa had shown. "Pam's human. When you sniffed her out as your mate, did you...?"

He already knew what TJ had ended up doing to convince the woman that werewolves existed. The situation was now legend in the pack.

"What are you not saying? Did you find your mate? Is she human?" TJ demanded.

Dead silence. Mark discovered he'd turned to face the paddle wheeler, searching instinctively for a glimpse of Tessa. "Yes, I found her. No, she's not human. She's...well, a cat. Not sure what kind yet."

He should have expected the laughter that greeted his announcement. TJ hooted for a moment before pulling himself together. "Congrats. Awesome news—the finding-your-mate part. You've been looking for her, you should be happy now. And at least you don't have to explain to her shifters exist."

There was a bright spot. "Good point."

"So why are you calling me instead of burning up the sheets? Something's got to be off."

Mark moved down the deck until he could peer in the windows, watching her blonde hair bounce as she followed Grampa Josiah's more stately march. They walked through the room Gramps used when he stayed overnight. Her smile seemed genuine while she listened to the old shifter, her gaze darting everywhere.

Was he in love with her? Damn it, what was love to a shifter? This feeling of intense satisfaction he had inside at having found her was a kind of love, wasn't it?

"Dude...you still there?" TJ clicked his tongue. "Let me guess. She's not from around here."

He didn't want to turn this into a guessing game. "She's a cat. She wants to fall in love before we mate."

This time silence echoed from the other end for way too long. TJ finally whistled softly. "Oh boy. Okay, I take it back how explaining about shifters was harder than what you've got. You mean she wants you to *wait*?"

"Seems that way. Yes."

"Well, hell."

They both sighed at the same time.

"That's why I called." There had to be something he could do to speed things along. "Maybe it would help if Pam had a heart-to-heart with her, because you two hit it off pretty fast, and all."

"I'll ask her. Hate to say it, my big bro is your best bet. Or Robyn. They know all kinds of things. And if you're serious, and you're going to bring her to visit the pack, you'd better talk to them anyway. I don't think tossing a cat into the mix is a good idea without checking with the Alphas first. Humans aren't cats. Like...whoa, your mate is a *cat*. Not saying I'd be too worried about... Well, you should just call them."

If there was an indication this situation was not normal, it was TJ warning him about how dangerous things could get. "Great. My one competitor for the 'picks the most awkward mate ever' award, and you're not very reassuring."

TJ laughed. "Don't worry. It'll all be worth it in the end.

She's your mate, dude. There's nothing like a mate, no matter how hairy the trip is to get to the point you're both one hundred percent in line. Trust me on that one."

It was all he had to go on. "Thanks, anyway."

"Dude?" TJ cut in one last time. "She's a cat. Think about it. This might not be as bad as you expect."

Mark had no idea what TJ was implying. He clicked off the phone and tried not to stare as Tessa wandered through his bedroom, expression of rapt adoration on her face as she peered at the woodwork.

At least she liked his house.

Standing outside staring in at her, his wolf demanding he go in and jump her bones, Mark came to a startling conclusion. Maybe TJ hadn't given him any long-term solutions to their problem, but one thing he had mentioned in passing was absolute truth.

It was going to be worth it in the end. She wanted him to fall in love with her? He was already over halfway there. Instinct wouldn't let him do anything but want her, *and* want the best for her.

If finding out all about her was what she required, then he was more than willing to become the most attentive student ever. Everything she longed for, everything she'd done. He would go back to school, and the only thing he'd concentrate on was her.

He was going to get a graduate degree in Tessa Williams, and he was all for fast-tracking the course of study. Even his wolf approved of his plans, and for the first time in the past hour the two sides of his psyche were in agreement.

School was in, starting now.

4

———

$\mathcal{T}$essa lowered her fork to the table and sighed contentedly. "That was delicious. Thank you."

Across from her Mark nodded, reaching for her plate. "Thirds?"

Tempting. Very tempting. Mark had managed to whip up a seafood lasagna in the matter of an hour while she'd explored the paddle wheeler inside and out. But even a good thing could be too much. "I can't eat another bite without exploding. Let me help with the dishes."

Gramps waved at them from his position at the head of the table. "You two go do your talking. I'm going to earn my keep and be chore boy tonight."

"Thanks, Gramps." Mark carried the dirty plates to the counter for him then nodded toward the office. "We do need to make a few decisions."

Tessa followed him, pleased to see the comfortable relationship between the two of them. "Your grampa is a lovely man."

Mark pulled out a chair for her. "He's stubborn, bossy and impulsive. I figured you'd like him."

She laughed. "Oh, you're learning about me that quickly, are you?"

The heat in his eyes was enough to raise the temperature in the room by several degrees. "I have a very good reason to want to know everything about you."

Well now. Tessa worked hard to stop from fidgeting in her chair, the heat between her legs somewhat unexpected, but nice to experience. He was turning her on without touching her. Interesting revelation.

Professional concerns first. "I know we have another issue to deal with, but can we step back and discuss the business side of things first?"

Mark nodded. "No problem. It's simpler now than it would have been. You want to buy the house—correct?"

"Yes, for the B&B and to offer eco-tours."

"I can't sell. Not unless you want to build an entire new building on this site."

What? "I want the paddle wheeler as the base. It's what makes the setting so spectacular."

"I agree. You've got a great idea, and I think it's going to work out well. Fact is, though, I literally *can't* sell you the place. The paddle wheeler is grandfathered—as long as the title remains with my family, it can stay. Once ownership passes to a new family, the boat has to be torn down, and any new buildings need to meet the building specs for the area."

Tessa's heart fell. "Oh no. You didn't mention that in your letter."

He smiled. "Stop looking so glum. That's what I said *would* happen. To avoid that option, I had proposed we go into business together. I remain owner of the house, you rent from me, together we run the place."

The idea had merit. But wait. "You said 'had'. Are you proposing something else?"

Mark turned toward her, lifting her hand in his. "You said you need me to go slower. That you won't accept we're mates right here and right now. I hate the idea, but fine, I see your point. In the meantime there's no reason we have to slow down on other plans."

Tessa stared at their linked hands. He rubbed his thumb over the back of her knuckles, the caress making lovely little hormones come to life and her body tingle. "What other plans?"

"Do you think there's a reason why we won't be mates eventually? I can't think of any. So I'm going to go ahead with that assumption and follow it to its logical conclusion. This is now your home. We can work together to make the B&B a reality. I'm a great builder and caretaker—all the renovations we need to do I'll complete over the winter."

The tingling edge of excitement was more from his touch than from his suggestion. "Not a business deal?"

"We'll write it up legally, of course. That's best for us in the long run anyway. I'll put up the paddle wheeler as my contribution to our partnership. You put up the money for the face-lift."

She was catching his vision. "Partners. I like the sound of that."

Only there were still some kinks to be worked out.

Mark stroked her arm, his touch making goose bumps rise. "It's a good way to begin our life together."

"Smooth talker." Tessa squirmed. Fine, she might have shut down the *mate, mate, mate* thingy, but that didn't mean the contact between them wasn't turning her on. "Couple questions. I had planned... Oh boy. Stop that."

Mark looked up from where he'd switched from petting her arm to stroking her leg. "Stop what?"

"That. You're touching me." Not that she minded, but...

"Sorry." He pulled his hands back and crossed his arms over his chest. "Not touching you is going to take some work on my part. I don't want to stop. Now, what did you have in mind?"

Tessa swallowed hard. He was doing something weird to her hormones. "I had planned on living in the house while renovations were going on."

He nodded. "Of course you'll live here. You've seen the upstairs is livable. If you draw up plans for what you want done on the other levels, I can get to work on them this week."

"I'll live here? You're okay with that?"

Mark's eyes flashed dark. "I wouldn't dream of you living anywhere else."

Suspicion snuck in. "And where are you going to live?"

"Here. With you."

That's what she'd figured. "Where, exactly, do you think I'm going to sleep?"

"With me."

Tessa sighed. "What part of 'not mates' do you not understand?"

Mark growled at her. A low, rumbly noise that made her inner cat sit up and preen. "You go around kissing everyone out of the blue the first time you meet them?"

What? "Oh, outside." Tessa shrugged. "I thought it was some kind of Alaskan greeting ritual."

He leaned in closer. "You like sex, right?"

Her cat answered faster than the human side. She was straddling his lap, licking the side of his neck in two seconds flat. Hmmm, salty and delicious. She could go for—

Mark dragged his hands down her back until he could hang on to her hips, his grip nearly wrapping around her. "You won't be kissing anyone else like that anymore. You want to go slow with the forever part of this—I'll give you that. But unless you want to be celibate for the next however long it takes for us to fall in love...?"

Oh dear. Tessa pulled back and gazed into his eyes. "I'm not some kind of hussy who can't control myself."

"I didn't think you were. But you're a cat. You're a shifter. When you need some satisfaction on the physical side, look no further than me. Consider me your own personal cat nip."

He used her hips to pull her higher, and her core slipped over the very solid ridge in his jeans. "Oh, my."

His voice dropped a notch. "I won't bite you until you say I can. But I will be there for you. Here at the B&B. While you explore your new home town..."

"Will you take me to visit the pack?" That would be the ultimate in acceptance, or so she'd heard.

He never even paused. "...when we meet the pack. I'll be there for you everywhere, including in bed."

His pupils dilated as she watched. An eerie but cool sensation snuck over her. It seemed her trip to the north had become more complicated than she'd imagined.

Soft, sweet-smelling woman in his lap, a plan in place for the future. While he hated that she'd said no to being mates right now, Mark couldn't fault her for anything else.

Only if they didn't move, he was going to have a tough time not acting on his wolf's urgings to strip her down and take her right there in his office.

A loud bark rang from the doorway, and they both turned to face his Gramps, who had shifted to his wolf and now paced around the chair they occupied.

Tessa stiffened. "Oops?"

"Don't worry. He's a wolf. He knows what's going on. Well, most of it." Mark leaned over and waved. "You heading back to the lodge?"

His Gramps dipped his chin, yipped a couple times. His final howl echoed off the walls as he headed out the door and left them alone.

"He said it was great meeting you, and he hopes to see you soon." Mark refrained from interpreting the rest of the old man's comments to Tessa. She didn't need to know what else his grandfather had suggested.

Then again, she was a shifter. She probably knew.

Tessa leaned away until her arms were fully stretched out. "So. Now what?"

"Now we get you settled." Mark couldn't wait to have her things in his place. Their scents mixing together, as well as a visible sign of them as a couple. "After that you can tell me what you've got in mind for the other floors, and I'll do some preliminary drafts so we can get started on renovations."

She tilted her head. "You are a most interesting person. Does nothing faze you? I mean, I tossed a lot at you today, and yet you seem so calm and relaxed. How do you do that?"

"Good genes."

Tessa smiled. "I'd noticed that as well."

She leaned in and brushed her lips against his cheek before crawling off his lap and tugging him upward. "I think your plan is awesome. And thank you. I'd far prefer to live here than at some hotel. We can have all kinds of fun together as we work on the project."

Fun. Oh goody. "Sounds great." He forced out the words. Really? Fun?

Damn.

She took off down the stairs like she was jet propelled. Mark followed more leisurely. If she was happy running at high RPM, who was he to try to change her?

Although, when he opened the front door and discovered she'd already returned with an armload of luggage, he wondered. "How do you move so fast?"

She sparkled at him. "Good genes, I guess."

Mark snorted. "You want everything inside?"

Tessa nodded. "You sure I should put my things in your bedroom? I could...clean up one of the rooms on—"

A snarl escaped without warning, and her cat eyes blinked rapidly as she stepped away.

Drat. "So much for my calm. Tessa, don't push the wolf, okay? Not now. Yes, my bedroom. Even suggesting anything else pisses him off."

"Sure. I can do that."

Poof. She was gone again. Up the stairs with only the swirl of her scent lingering on the air to torment him.

Mark went for another load, wondering how long it would take for his dual personalities of shifter/human to have a major breakdown.

He unloaded everything, carrying it into the main entrance before locking up and taking the first stack all the way upstairs. Rounding the corner into his bedroom, his heart was already racing at the idea of finding her in there. His mate, part of his future...as soon as he discovered more about her.

She wasn't there.

Neither was she in the bathroom or the living room or the kitchen. He'd just about given up when a flash of blonde hair drew his attention to the balcony.

She sat on the railing, happily kicking her feet as she stared over the ocean.

His heart rate tripled. Mark opened the outside door cautiously, making sure he didn't spook her. It was a long, *long* way down if she fell.

"Tessa?" He spoke softly. "What are you doing?"

She twisted her head to flash him a brilliant smile. "Sunset colours are so pretty tonight. Come..." She patted the spot next to her. "Watch with me."

He strolled over, leaned on the railing and casually slipped his arm around her waist to make sure he had her anchored. Only then did he start to breathe again. "Very pretty sunsets from here."

"We'll set up drinks and snacks in the evening for the B&B guests. They can sit here and talk about how wonderful their day was, and then new people will want to go on the same trips, and it'll work in a circle. More happy visitors coming all the time."

She leaned her head against his shoulder and sighed contentedly.

"I think this is the first time since we met you haven't been moving at a breakneck pace," Mark pointed out. The sensation of her in his arms was so right. He dragged in breath after breath of her scent in an attempt to satisfy his cravings.

A yawn escaped, and she stretched, teetering precariously toward the wrong side of the railing. "Sunsets do that to me. Soporific effect? Is that right?"

He stepped behind her and caught hold tighter. "If that

means you're ready to curl up in front of the fire, I'm good with it."

"I like fires." Her voice slipped into lower, sleepy tones that tickled along his spine and promised slumbering kitty within minutes.

Then she sent him into near panic mode as she twirled in his grasp, her arms around his neck the only thing stopping her from tumbling to the ground many feet below them.

Mark held in the swear words that wanted to escape, instead lifting her over the railing until he could settle her more comfortably in his arms. He moved to a safer position, heading toward the house before he glanced down at her face.

Her eyes were closed, her long eyelashes resting against her cheeks. Her mouth pulled into a slight pucker, and a tiny sound escaped her lips. She snuggled up to his chest, breathing rhythmically.

She'd already fallen asleep.

Mark carried her to his bed, depositing her on the mattress before stepping back to debate what came next.

Stripping her down seemed...dirty. If she'd been awake, he could have asked her what she wanted, but there was a line he refused to cross now that she'd drawn it in the sand.

Instead, he pulled off her shoes, put them on the floor in the closet. She'd hung up a bunch of her things, and he smiled at the sight.

When he turned back to the bed, it was to discover she'd nestled into the covers, curled up and purring.

Seriously purring.

Mark sat on the edge of the mattress next to her, and stared. Rosy colour in her cheeks, one hand lying comfortably beside her head, the other stretched out toward where he intended to crawl in later.

To a human it might have seemed strange—that she'd said no to mating with him and yet was snuggled into his bed. Made sense to him, though. There was a huge difference between sex for fun and sex as mates and plain old cuddling. He wasn't as sure about cats, but wolves were pack animals. Being with others satisfied something deep inside.

So far, so good. As long as he could keep them moving in the proper direction.

They'd discussed many ideas for the B&B, but she'd never promised to stay forever. Until she did, he wouldn't be able to calm down, even though she'd admired his supposed placid exterior. Inside he was a bundle of concerns, wanting more. Needing more. One step at a time, he had to convince her they belonged together.

The sound rising from her increased—that cute little cross between a snore and a purr, and Mark smiled.

There was another thing he could add to the list of things he knew about his mate. She had two speeds: full and off. He grabbed a light quilt from the cupboard and covered her up for the night.

5

*E*yes wide open.

Ouch.

Eyes snapping shut in self-defence as sunshine hit her face. Tessa threw back the covers and leapt to her feet.

When the floor didn't seem familiar, it took a few seconds to complete the mental whirl through everything that had happened the previous day. She glanced down, spotting the well-wrinkled clothing she'd slept in at the same moment she caught sight of Mark.

He was asleep, sitting upright in an oversized wingback chair, his temple resting against one support.

Her gaze darted over the room, taking in the messed-up bed sheets, her disheveled condition and his awkward sleeping arrangements.

She hadn't meant to kick him out of his own bed.

Guess that conversation would have to happen today. She slipped into the bathroom, washed her face, admired the view out the window then shot herself into the kitchen to discover what he might have in the fridge. She needed something she could pull together for breakfast without ruining the food, burning the house down or poisoning them both.

Cereal and milk. That she could handle. Digging through the cupboard turned up bowls, spoons and cups. Which made her think of coffee.

Cofffeeeeeeeeeee.

She ignored the little warning twinges her brain shot at her. While she didn't need coffee, it was clear from the impressive machine sitting on the counter that Mark wouldn't mind a cup. After being rude enough to keep him from a good night's sleep, the polite thing was to do a little extra work on his behalf. He would probably love to have a nice cup of joe to wake up to.

Tessa dragged the silver and black monstrosity away from the wall to look it over. Seemed simple enough. She pulled a lever, and a small compartment opened up, the scent of ground beans making her toes curl.

Nope, not a good idea, sniffing anything stimulating. She'd learned that back in college after a particularly horrifying event involving Red Bull, chocolate and an all-night study session.

But for Mark? She'd find a way to escape the buzz she could get just preparing a pot.

A bit of digging through the freezer brought up a bag of small dark ovals. She hurried to avoid getting more of a head rush than necessary. She loaded the hopper, closed the lever and pushed the big red button. A satisfying whirl filled the air.

Between the cranking noises and the bubbling she soon had going, Tessa was pleased.

Transferring the ground beans into the little cup holder she was sure she'd seen people on television use, she paused. Something didn't seem right. A bright flashing light distracted her from her misgivings and she rushed ahead and flicked the final switch.

Dark liquid poured from the machine's spout. And continued to pour. She grabbed another cup and watched anxiously as it approached the point of overflowing as well. Tessa scrambled in the cupboard and pulled out as many cups as she could reach, falling in to a comfortable routine of slipping one cup after another under the unending drip.

Pulling the power cord might have seemed desperate, but soon it was her only choice. She'd run out of cups.

Tessa ignored the mess and picked up the original coffee, stirring one final time to add a pretty swirl to the foam.

Her attempt resulted in something closer to a fish head than a flower. She shrugged off her disappointment and headed to the bedroom. Mark would appreciate the gesture. She was sure of it.

He was still in the chair, eyelids fluttering as she approached. His smile brightened, his gaze taking her in. "Hey."

She put the cup down on the side table and dropped to her knees beside him, hands resting on his thighs. "Hey yourself. You silly puppy. Why didn't you come to bed properly?"

Mark stretched. "You were in the middle of the bed, and I didn't want to bother you or make you uncomfortable."

"Awwww." Something went soft and squishy inside. "That's so sweet of you. Unnecessary, but sweet."

"It's not silly to want the best for you," Mark insisted. "Don't ask me to not do what I think is right."

He'd got her on that one. "You could have slept in the other room."

He shook his head. "Nope. Wolf wouldn't let me."

Tessa paused. "I'm sorry. I'm making your life awkward, aren't I?"

"Thrown my world for a loop. It's okay, though." Mark sat up to the edge of the chair and patted her hand gently. "I'll live."

Now she was even happier she'd found a way to do something nice for him this morning. "I made you coffee."

He took a deep breath and...cringed? "Really? Umm, thank you."

He picked up the cup and brought it to his nose to take another, more cautious sniff.

"Is something wrong?"

"No, not at all." Mark blinked hard. He put the cup to his mouth and took a sip. His throat seemed to work hard as he swallowed. "Thank you," he repeated.

Only he held the mug and didn't drink anymore, just stared at her, a hint of a smile on his lips.

Nice-looking lips, she noted.

"Well. Plans for the day." She rose to her feet and snuck to the closet, shifting a few garments around. "You have a couple drawers for me to use?"

He put his cup down and followed her, pulling open a space and removing the T-shirts. "Have at 'er. If you need more room, I'll build you your own dresser."

"Awesome." She stripped off her dirty clothing and reached for clean undies, stopping when this strange gurgling noise met her ears. She straightened and looked at him with concern. "Mark, you okay?"

His pupils were huge, his nostrils flaring. The tension in his body screamed out, if she'd happened to miss the fists clenched at his sides. "No worries."

Deep and low, his voice whispered through barely opened lips.

She pulled on panties and adjusted her bra, tugging the closet open to grab a fresh pair of jeans. "What would you like to do this morning?"

No answer.

She twirled to find him gone. A quick flash of a leg showed he'd stepped into the bathroom. The water turned on and she paced over to peek inside. "Mark, what—?"

He stood fully clothed under the shower, his head resting against the tiles. "Yes?"

Okay, that was a little strange. She supposed that was one way to get the wrinkles out of slept-in clothing. "Umm, when you're done. No rush."

She tiptoed out, trying not to disturb him.

After all, he'd had a hard night.

MARK WAS GOING TO DIE. No, dying would be the simple solution. A lack of oxygen to his body would mean blood would stop rushing through his veins. It would mean his cock would stop turning into a heat-seeking missile as far as Tessa was concerned.

He'd been so careful last night, maintaining boundaries that would give her space. And this morning, trying to act normal, like he would around any other shifter he wasn't itching to get intimate with.

The whole shifter lack of shyness had backfired in a big way. He now knew from a very up-close-and-personal glance the following details: his mate was a natural blonde. She had freckles. She was more than a mouthful.

He turned the water temperature down a notch hoping

to quench a few of the internal fires, but it was little use. He was hard. Capital H hard and staying that way.

The only way to survive this crazy situation was going to be exhausting labour. If he was too tired to get it up, he might endure the coming weeks.

He pulled himself from the shower and dressed, no sign of his adorably hyper cat anywhere. Well, at least not until he walked into his kitchen. The disaster area proved what the earlier cup of coffee had hinted at. If he didn't want to be poisoned, he needed to ban her from cooking.

Which was fine. He liked to cook. Mark pulled the coffee maker forward and grimaced at the sight of ground fava beans in the hopper. His disgust switched to amusement when he spotted the cereal she'd left for him on the table. Her bowl was used and empty, his all ready for the milk to be poured. What made it extraordinary was she'd folded a napkin into the shape of a swan and left it waiting for him.

Mark ate quickly, threw out the multiple cups of loathsome *not coffee* liquid and loaded the dishwasher. Then he went looking for his mate.

He found her on the main floor, surrounded by papers. Mark stood silently observing as she skimmed a pencil over the notepad, her fingers flying across the page. She tore off the top piece of paper and added it to a pile on her right.

"You going to stand there all morning?" Tessa smiled at him.

He paced over to stare down at her chaos. "You've been busy."

She wrinkled her nose. "Sorry about the mess upstairs. I'll clean it up before lunch, but I had an inspiration for the layout down here and wanted to get it on paper before I lost my train of thought."

Mark resisted making any smart-ass comments about trains running amuck through the house, instead squatting to examine the top page of a pile. The details of the drawing shocked him. "Holy cow, Tessa. Did you do these all this morning?"

She nodded, shifting her weight as she pointed in a circle. "Design plans for main floor and second floor. Slight modifications to the third, just a few things to make it easier for a B&B setup. I hope you don't mind."

He was too stunned to be upset. They weren't just bubble diagrams, with rough "bathroom goes here" type notes, but full-out plans with measurements and everything. Mark shuffled through the fourth pile resting at his feet. "These are furniture designs."

"For the guest rooms. That stack is for the couple rooms, the next for the dorms. I wanted to see what you thought before planning for family rooms. You want to have kids around the place, or not?"

Mark ignored her question for a moment as he lowered himself to the floor. "How on earth did you do all this so fast?" He gawked at the pages. "Plus, you're spot-on accurate. You've got measurements for the rooms—where are you hiding your measuring tape?"

"It's built in." She grinned and tapped her temple. "I can eyeball a room and know the dimensions at a glance. It's not a very handy skill except when it comes to designing. Or parking... I can parallel park in spaces that would make your hair stand on end."

Holy shit. He set down the stack and went for the next one, again amazed at the details and simple beauty of what she suggested. "I think your ideas are brilliant. You accomplished enough in an hour to keep me busy for the next four months."

"I'll help," Tessa offered. "I can swing a hammer, and I don't mind getting dirty."

Mark exchanged the drawings for her hands, holding her tight. "I'm...impressed. And pleased."

Tessa beamed. And wiggled.

He examined her more closely, trying to figure out how she was moving in such a strange way. "Tessa, what are you sitting on?"

"A balance board. Gives my body something to concentrate on while I'm doing things with my hands. Keri came up with the idea when we were in college. She's my bestie. You know her? Of course you do, she mated with Jared in July. I think she said she'd be back in the fall."

"I've met her." Well, a point in his favour—his mate already had a friend in the pack. "We can meet up with her and Jared, if they're around. Why don't you call to find out?"

She shot to her feet, somehow continuing to balance on the tippy wooden plank as she dragged him upright with her. "I'd like that very much. You're so sweet."

Mark untangled himself to gather her work piles together. "We'll do a walk-through on these ideas after you get in touch with them."

"That would be great. Hey, you never told me what you prefer—family rooms or no?"

He'd been avoiding thinking about it, because the answer was all tangled together in his brain. The image of little kids running through the house led to thinking about *their* kids someday running through the house. Which led to images of Tessa being pregnant, which backtracked to full-colour, live-action feature-film-quality high-def sex scenes, starring her and him.

Although he was pretty sure porn would have nothing on the actual event. Not with them being mates.

Some time in the last minute he'd moved in closer, again, and when she squirmed on the board, her torso brushed his intimately. Mark swallowed hard. Ignored the instant response of his body. Forced the words out. "Kids are okay."

Tessa leapt into the air, wrapping her arms and legs around him. He dropped the papers to catch her, hands cradling her ass as she leaned forward until her lips pressed to his. He sucked in her taste like a starving man.

She rested their foreheads together, a contented smile lighting her face. "I think I like you."

"Well, that's good." Nothing was going to distract him from enjoying the temporary warmth of their bodies touching. He added a few more items to the list of what he knew about her. *Impulsive, but talented. Athletic.*

"I think we can accomplish some great things together," she announced. "We'll make an awesome team."

"A team?" He wasn't going to pass up this opportunity. "More than that, Tessa. We're mates. Our skills complement each other."

Her eyes went wide and she nodded slowly. "Cool. And you do like kids."

"I like you." It was enough for now.

She didn't seem to be in a hurry to get away, so he took total advantage and kissed her again. Nibbled on her lower lip as she hummed happily and tangled her fingers in his hair. Her mouth was so soft under his, her wonderful scent whispering through his entire body and somehow increasing his tension even as it satisfied him.

He licked the seam of her lips, and she snuck the tip of her tongue against his. Head rush followed, sensory overload. Mark got lost in the complete rightness that was his mate.

If stolen kisses were all he could get, he'd force the beast inside to accept them. He and Tessa would have forever together. If it took a few more days than usual to start on the journey, well, he had enough patience to make it through.

In the end, it would be worth it.

Mark savoured the kiss, the weight of her in his hands. The intimate contact between their bodies. He stored up all the sensations in the hopes his wolf wouldn't rebel and ruin his good intentions.

The beast grumbled, but settled, at least for now.

6
———

By the time dinner had rolled past, Tessa found herself strangely fatigued. She transferred the dirty dishes from the counter into the dishwasher, though, before standing and stretching her lower back.

"Sorry again about the mess I made this morning." There was no excuse for it. She wasn't some flighty teenager who needed to be cared for by mommy anymore. Her lack of consideration annoyed her.

She was a capable grown woman. She'd organized and run a cruise ship—and this morning she'd childishly left a disaster behind her?

Tessa straightened from her task and gasped in surprise at how close Mark was. He cupped her face and shook his head. "Stop apologizing. It wasn't a big deal. We've had a great day, very productive, and a few extra dishes have been forgotten. Okay?"

"Sure." Only guilt remained.

Her eyelids were heavy, and she was dog-tired, although that particular thought made her want to giggle.

His touch remained gentle on her skin. His thumb

caressed her cheek as he searched her eyes. "Let's get some fresh air. Would you like to go for a run?"

Her cat uncoiled like a spring, frantic relief washing her limbs. "Yes, oh, that would be marvelous."

Mark pushed between her shoulders and directed her toward the bedroom. "Strip and shift. I'll wait for you at the back door—it's set up so we can open it in either form."

"Wait."

He paused in the middle of turning away.

Tessa wasn't sure where the confusion inside had come from. Something wasn't right, but she couldn't imagine what it was.

"Tessa?"

She forced down the strange sensation and smiled. "Nothing. I'll meet you at the door in a minute."

Why did the silence in the room echo as she took off her clothes and set them aside? She glanced around, looking for a clue of what was making her so uneasy. Nothing twigged. Nothing made sense except her cat's increasing demands for that promised run *now*.

She walked naked through the kitchen, not wanting to shift in the bedroom. Her cougar curled upward, pushing at her skin, and she stopped at the top of the stairs and gave in. Let the shift come over her, limbs and muscles rearranging as she settled into her other form.

The usual rush of "feels good to shift" that was always a part of the transformation was so diluted she sat on her haunches for a moment in bewilderment.

Now the cat was more in control than the human, and the cougar wanted to keep moving. She slipped down the stairs, ignoring all the things that would have sidetracked her before, instead eager to get to the place she could be free to run.

Run with Mark. Her mate.

Tessa had imagined that thought would piss her cougar off far more than it did. The sight of Mark in full fur might have had something to do with the inner calm. Tessa wished she'd taken the time to examine him before she'd changed skins, because he was a beautiful animal, at least as far as a cat could appreciate a dog.

White muzzle, thick silver fur with black markings. He tipped his head at her before standing on his hind legs to reach the doorknob. The flat lever twisted under his touch, the door swung open, and he waited for her to slip out ahead of him.

He nudged the door closed with his forehead, then while she was getting her bearings, he brushed past her shoulder and took off.

The chase had begun.

Directly behind the paddle wheeler, they met wilderness. The back-fence line met the trees, so once they stepped over that point there was nothing but rolling foothills. Narrow but well-worn paths led through the underbrush, and Mark leapt from one to the next, always guiding them upward. The heat of day faded to be replaced by the cooler air clinging to the earth, trickling down from the heights.

Tessa pushed herself to catch him, the demand on her muscles finally surpassing the strange malaise that had waylaid her. Blood pumped, and her mind calmed, as if all the excess ideas flitting through her brain were used up in the mechanics of paws hitting the dirt.

He vanished from sight around a corner, and she put on a burst of speed to close the gap between them. She flew into a clearing and found herself tackled to the ground, his attack coming from the side.

Laughter bubbled up, the sheer joy of the cat relishing his playfulness as a wolf. He crawled off her and backed away, head low, tail wagging furiously.

She licked a paw and wiped it over her ears, grooming them back into order and knocking off the leaves that clung to her.

Mark's jaw opened, and his wolfie grin said it all. He thought she was being a typical cat, did he? Tessa ignored him and glanced around the clearing he'd brought her to, admiring the panorama visible on the leeward side of the hill.

The view from the paddle wheeler was gorgeous, but this was spectacular. The last rays of the sun fell in streaks, creating a spotlight effect over the field. Tessa didn't plan it, just reacted, heading for the nearest patch of sunshine and stretching lazily as warmth furled over her.

Another kind of heat hit her. Mark, rubbing his way along her side until he'd managed to wrap himself around her and clearly state his ownership. In her cat form, it was strange how little that idea bothered her.

The human, however, was the curious one. She bumped her nose against his muzzle before separating herself so she wouldn't hurt him. Then she shifted back, coming to her human skin at his side.

"So lovely." She ran her hand over his head and down his back, and Mark rumbled happily.

All the anxiety she'd felt earlier had dissipated, popping like bubbles, and Tessa went with her instincts. She stretched out on the thick layer of moss and rested her head on his soft furry back. The steady beat of his heart and the last heat of the sun lulled her to that point midway between sleeping and being awake.

~

SHE HAD HIM PINNED. Mark laid his chin on his forepaws and slowed his racing thoughts. Tessa's cat form was pretty cool. There would still be questions regarding the pack accepting her, but...

Time. Give it time. He breathed out through his nose and watched the tiny grasses in front of him sway.

The sun slid off them in less than ten minutes. While he hated to disturb her, they should head inside, especially since she was lying butt-naked in the bush. He twisted his head slowly, until he could see her face. Temptation beckoned.

Mark licked her, cheek to temple.

Her nose wrinkled as her eyes popped open, and she grinned. "Hey, none of that, or I'll catch you catnapping sometime and get my revenge."

She returned to her cougar form, and this time he let her set the pace, following to be sure she took the correct paths that would lead them home.

Home. The word made him happier now than it ever had.

Within half an hour they were in front of the fireplace, the kettle on the stove whistling softly. They'd both pulled on sweats, Tessa wearing a T-shirt from his drawer that satisfied the barest part of the hunger inside him.

When he slipped onto the couch, Tessa abandoned the easy chair she'd been curled up in while he worked, instead crawling into his lap and cuddling in tight.

Every muscle stiffened, every desire he had to take her roared back up to hundred percent.

"Thank you for the lovely run." She whispered the words against his neck. He caressed her, his hands going instinctively to tangle in her hair. Their drinks forgotten as he lifted her chin and kissed her.

Every time he touched her, it was easier to wait, and harder. Easier, because it was just so damn right. Mentally he was on board.

Physically? There was the issue. Waiting became harder—harder like his cock, which pressed against her hip. She had to feel it as she sat in his lap, had to know how much she affected him.

He reined his desires in. Made himself stop drowning in her taste. Pulled her to his chest and worked to calm his breathing.

"Tell me something I don't know about you." He stroked her hair over her shoulder. "Tell me about a dream you have—what you want to accomplish."

Because while he wanted her, he wanted it all. And the sooner he filled his brain with All About Tessa, the better.

She sat up, head tilted as she looked him in the eye. "I want to feel like a success at something."

The strange way she'd emphasized her words forced Mark to think through her comment before responding. "Don't you mean *be* a success?"

Tessa shook her head. "I..." She paused. "I am successful. I've got a great education, a supportive family who runs a business I got to contribute to—and I didn't screw up too badly in the end. From an outside-looking-in point of view, I think people see me and assume I've got it all together."

He'd thought so. "But you don't feel like that's true?"

The bright amusement usually present in her face was missing, as was the squirming he'd already grown to expect. "If things work out well, but I didn't do anything to make it happen, should I feel successful? Dumb luck isn't something to be admired, Mark."

Oh hell. "This is why the mating thing feels off to you, right? Why you want me to know about you and care about you before we make it official?"

"Mating's got to be the purest form of dumb luck there is." Tessa stroked a finger over his brow, rubbing away the tension. "It's not wrong, but it's just not right. It's so… generic. Why does your wolf want *me*?"

Because it *was* right. They belonged together, but simply saying the words wasn't going to convince her.

Besides, she had a point, even though those kind of things usually worked themselves out later with wolves. "Thank you for sharing. I'm honoured you trusted me."

She snorted lightly. "Too honest for my own good, at times."

"I had that on the list I'm making," Mark said. Her brows went up and he hurried to reassure her. "Not the *too*-honest bit, but the honest part. I like that you don't avoid issues, Tessa. It's a good way to be. Keeps things in the open, makes it easier for me to fix my mistakes when I blow it with you down the road."

That brought a smile to her face. "You sure you're going to be the one to screw up? Seems so far I'm the one dropping bombs left, right and center in this relationship."

"So you admit this is a relationship?"

She poked him in the chest and leaned in closer. "I'm sitting in your lap telling you my deepest, darkest secrets. You'd better believe this is more than casual, buddy. I like dating."

"Is it dating when it's with your mate?" He wasn't going to let her forget where this was headed.

"Hmmm, whatever we want to call it is fine."

Her hands floated down his chest, fingertips tickling his sensitive skin, making him ache. The distance between them disappeared and their mouths connected again. Slow, thorough kisses that made his limbs loosen and other parts tighten.

He returned the favour, stroking her back. Her waist. Sneaking a hand up over her belly until he cupped one breast in his palm. Her nipple tightened, poking against the fabric of the T-shirt she wore.

The entire time she kissed him, exploring with her tongue, letting him nip at her lips. He broke away to press a line of kisses along her jaw until he could catch hold of her earlobe and suck it into his mouth.

Her full-body shiver was more than enough reward.

"Tessa. Let me..." If he was going to beg, what should he beg for? Small steps forward meant he wouldn't get what he wanted, which was to drive her crazy until she'd had a half dozen orgasms before burying himself in her and marking her thoroughly.

She grabbed the bottom of the shirt she wore and stripped it away. Her naked breasts popped into view, and all thoughts of begging fled, swallowed by raging need.

TESSA BIT BACK HER LAUGHTER. She was turned on and eager to play, but the expression on Mark's face right now? Sheer puppy-dog eyes. Although she'd be nice and refrain from making that comment out loud.

Wolves could be sensitive about such things.

She'd planned on acting a little coy, flirting and showing off. She'd forgotten one vital bit of information. She had been teasing him all day.

He caught hold of her hips and suddenly she was airborne, lifted over his lap and held so she looked down at him as he stared eye level with her breasts. Anticipation built as he remained stationary.

"You seem unsure what to do next." Tessa smoothed her palms over his head.

His gaze lifted the short distance needed to make direct contact with hers. "I know what to do, but I'm savouring."

"Like a steak?"

"No objections on my part to eating you all up."

"You big, bad wolf—*oooh*!"

He'd obviously stopped savouring because warm lips wrapped around her nipple. Mark sucked, and tingling lines of pleasure radiated out to steal around her torso. A moment's reprieve came as he switched sides, licking firmly, his tongue rasping over the delicate tip. His grip on her hips remained tight enough to direct her where he wanted, yet the tender caress of his thumbs added to the erotic torment.

One side, then the other. Tessa closed her eyes and did her own savouring. The tenderness in his touch remained, but the urgency was there as well. Increased breathing, heart rates rising. Without taking his lips from her skin, he adjusted their position and made contact with the edge of her panties.

She shivered at the sensation. He played along the seam, back and forth, brushing his knuckles over the center of her sex the same moment he closed his teeth on her nipple.

Direct line hit, pleasure fast overtaking her. He'd barely begun touching the really good bits, and she was poised to go off. A little firmer now, his fingers slipped under the material and separated her folds.

Mark hummed in approval. "So wet. Let me make you feel good."

She would have agreed, yet she couldn't say anything. Just a long, low catlike purr she'd have been self-conscious of except he'd found her clit.

Embarrassed? Only by how quickly she was going to climax.

He petted her with his fingertips, keeping his attention focused on the sensitive spot. Intense pleasure rose faster, egged on when he returned to kissing her breasts. Tessa held her breath as the moment hit, the pulse of her core shooting all kinds of incredible chemicals throughout her body. She clutched his head to her chest and rocked with delight.

He supported her until she stopped shaking, his right hand caressing everywhere he could. Her hips, her back, up her rib cage with a delicate whisper. Tessa drew in a deep breath and smiled contentedly at him.

Then she raised a brow and licked her lips. "My turn..."

There could be no mistaking the eager hope in his eyes. Tessa slipped backward off his lap, running her hands up his thighs. This time it was her turn to explore him. To see what he enjoyed and ease a little of the tension in his strong body. She tugged at his T-shirt, and it vanished between one second and the next.

Eager indeed.

The large bulge behind his sweats was unmistakable. She took a lesson from what he'd done, though, and when she leaned forward it was to press her lips to his solid abdomen.

Mark groaned.

She licked along the ridges of his muscles, taking her time and working her way downward inch by inch.

He growled. A long, low sound similar enough to what she'd done earlier, she knew exactly what it meant.

She lifted her head, timing it just right so she could enjoy his reaction to her fingers closing over his hard length. Satisfaction at seeing his eyes roll back struck at the same moment a peculiar sound echoed through the house. Kind of like a door slamming.

Mark's eyes snapped open.

Singing rose from somewhere faraway. On the main floor? Getting closer. A sea shanty, one with a lot of slurred words and yet high enthusiasm.

Fingers closed around her wrists as Mark pulled her hands from his groin, his breathing uneven but getting steadier. "We have to stop."

"But—"

She accepted the T-shirt he returned, slipping it over her head as she watched in confusion. He took a deep breath and rose to his feet, wincing for a few steps as if he were in pain.

The singing grew louder and Tessa clued in. "Oh."

Mark adjusted himself and winked at her. "*Oh* is right."

He pulled his shirt on before making his way to the top of the stairwell. They waited without a word, instead exchanging snorts of laughter until his grandfather appeared.

The man gave an extra lusty finish to his chorus before slapping Mark on the back and turning to face her.

"Well, lovely to see you again, dear. Ready for the trip? Got everything you need?"

She didn't get a chance to answer before Mark spoke. "Of course she's ready. Will you be taking us out soon, sir?"

He guided the older wolf into the living room and settled him in a well-worn leather rocker.

"We leave with the tide. Heard the weather's going to change—we'll want to get past the narrows on full swells."

Mark nodded curtly. "Yes, sir."

Gramps fell silent, staring into the fire. Mark sat back on the couch and reached out a hand to Tessa. She curled up at his side. The sexual tension between them lingered, and she'd already had an orgasm. She couldn't imagine what Mark felt like.

His lips pressed to her temple. "Stop worrying. Everything is okay."

He spoke softly, so she matched his volume. "Were you expecting him tonight?"

Mark laughed, stroking his fingers through her hair. "I think you know the answer to that by what he interrupted."

Gramps fumbled with his pipe, humming his tune now as he worked to get the tobacco lit. Then he sat back and smiled, rocking as he gazed into the flames, an aromatic cloud surrounding him.

His appearance wasn't scary or anything, just unexpected. Tessa's curiosity shot to high.

Mark touched her cheek, bringing her attention to him. "He gets...confused. This was his ship, and there are times he kind of goes back in time. I don't know when he's going to show up, which is part of the reason I've never sold the place."

"But you can't sell it."

Mark took a deep breath and nodded, his turn to stare at the fire. "I could sell the place as land alone, but what would happen then? Gramps is happy at the seniors' lodge except for those occasional moments he loses track of what year it is. He comes, spends a few nights, then he seems to wake up and heads home. I can't imagine what would happen if he showed up during a session to discover the paddle wheeler was gone. He'd be devastated. Think they'd left without him or something."

Gramps continued to rock while Mark's confession rocked her. "You've been staying for his sake."

"He's my family." Mark smiled indulgently at his grandfather. "He's the reason I missed being on the cruise ship with you in the spring—I had a position with the maintenance crew, you know. The person who'd promised to house sit for me while I was away never showed up that morning. You sailed before I could make other arrangements."

Another mystery solved. "Keri and Jared didn't mind how that turned out."

They sat in comfortable silence for a while—well, relaxed as Mark could be. Tessa leaned her head on his shoulder and whispered, "We could go to bed..."

His nostrils flared for a moment. "Tempting, but I'd better make sure he settles for the night."

He stood and brought her to her feet as well, kissing her before tucking a loose strand of hair behind her ear. "Go to bed. I'll see you later."

Tessa crawled under the covers feeling even more confused than when Mark had first announced they were mates. She attempted to stay awake until he came in so they could finish what they'd started, or at least have time to talk.

Only the soft pillow lulled her, and the next thing she knew the sunshine was announcing the start of another day.

7

———

Monday

Gramps made them breakfast before breaking out a mop and "swabbing the decks".

Mark excused himself shortly after that. "I'm going to run into town and stop by the permit office to see what kind of timeline we're looking at. You can come with me if you're interested."

For some reason the idea of heading out didn't excite her the way it usually did. "You go on. I'm itching to explore the place a little more. Work on a few brochure ideas."

He stared at her for a moment before cupping the back of her neck and pulling her against him for a brief, intense kiss. They separated, her lips tingling, his pupils gone dark. He stroked her cheek. "If you think of anything you need, make a list."

The door closed behind him, and something very uncomfortable trailed up her spine leaving her listless. Edgy.

She wandered the bottom two floors for a while,

picturing the changes she'd drawn all being completed. The place was going to be gorgeous when it was finished. She nabbed a stack of sticky notes and popped information on the walls that she wanted to remember to discuss with Mark when he got back.

The beam of sunshine falling through the window had to be the reason she blinked in surprise half an hour later as she woke up from a catnap. She didn't remember going back to his bedroom, though, or putting on the shirt that smelt like him.

It took her full concentration to manage a bit of computer work before Mark returned with supplies for the kitchen and a pile of mail-order shopping catalogues.

She flicked through the pile quickly. Decorative lighting, specialty fixtures. "Oh, nice."

Mark smiled as he sat down to the submarine sandwiches she'd put together while the groceries had been unpacked. "I figured you'd like something to hold on to, rather than just shopping online."

"That's so sweet of you. Thanks."

"No problem. Also, good news on the renovation front. One of the pack works in the permits department, and I got to speak to him." Mark nodded thanks at Gramps as the older man refilled their glasses. "He'll make sure the forms are pushed through fast for us. Which doesn't mean we can get away with any funny business in the important things, but it does mean we can go ahead and start immediately."

Tessa sat in shocked silence.

Mark grinned wider. "What's the matter, cat got your tongue?"

She slipped out her tongue at him for a second before shaking her head. "You're kidding. We can start on the renovations now?"

"I've got the first load of wood being delivered this afternoon, and a dumpster box. We can clean out the unusable material and dive right in. I asked a few of the pack to help with the hard labour."

She wasn't sure how to respond. "That's incredible. When I arranged my flights, I thought we'd spend weeks in negotiations before anything would get underway."

"No reason to wait. I told you that. This is your home, so why not begin making your dreams come true?" He caught her fingers in his and squeezed them lightly. "Happy?"

"More than I can tell you."

Gramps leaned back in his chair. "Going to spiff up the place, are you? Sounds like a plan. Bit of spit and polish always a good thing. Shall I move my gear to the crew's quarters?"

"You're fine where you are, Gramps." Mark winked at Tessa so his grandfather didn't see it.

She melted a little inside at the care in Mark's voice. A yawn overtook her, and she blinked in surprise. Again? "Well, I don't know where that came from."

Mark shrugged. "If you'd like to take a nap for a bit, we'll have time to talk about things later."

She should've argued with him. If the work was going to start on the B&B, she wanted to be there. But her eyes wouldn't stay open, and if it hadn't been for Mark's strong clasp around her, she would have curled up right there at the table. He tucked her into bed and sat for a moment, skimming his hands over her shoulders and head.

"I like you, Mr. Weaver." She managed to whisper the words before sleep overtook her for the second time that day.

"You're going to love me," he said firmly.

Or maybe she just imagined it.

Tuesday

SHOCKED by the sight of ten a.m. flashing on the clock beside the bed, Tessa dragged herself to vertical. She lingered in the shower for thirty minutes in an attempt to wake up.

When she did find her way downstairs, it was to discover building materials stacked in neat rows on the main floor, the old timbers already removed and piled high in the dumpster outside.

A note fluttered on the back of the door, and she strolled over to read it.

Taking Gramps home. Call if you need me.

Her nose twitched, and her cat complained that he was gone. She had her phone in her hand and the call going through before she'd thought it through.

"Morning, sleeping beauty."

"I'm so embarrassed. I feel as if I've gone narcoleptic or something. Did you even go to bed last night?" Tessa poked her head into what would be the far storage rooms. "How did you get everything cleared out so fast? I never heard a thing."

"I told you, guys from the pack came over to help."

She'd slept through it all, and that strange fact made her pause. Although on the good side? There was something positive to be said for the pack. "I hope you passed on my thanks."

"Of course." He shot back the words so quickly she wondered what was up, but only for a moment. Her cat was too busy examining the cleared-out spaces to be curious about a conversation.

"How's your grandfather?" she asked.

"He's great. Decided that the salmon run was more important than the paddle wheeler. He and his buddies are going out for a few days."

Which meant they'd be alone in the house. Tessa's mind raced with naughty possibilities. "Are you coming home?"

"As soon as I get Gramps settled. You go ahead and take it easy. We'll swing a hammer this afternoon."

Taking it easy sounded like a great idea. Except before she did, there was one thing she simply had to do. He'd worked like a dog—*ha!*—to get things ready for building, the least she could do was provide an edible meal. Emphasis on the edible part.

Between the computer, foodnetwork.com and a couple burnt fingers, she managed. Sheer determination forced her to keep muddling through as her cat, of all creatures, insisted she provide for...Mark.

Although she wasn't exactly sure *what* her cat was trying to tell her. The feline was all focused on images of sunshine and warm cozy pillows and lazy days by the fire.

Tessa shook her head. *Whoa.* That was weird. Maybe she'd been working too hard before she came to Haines, or something.

Her cat obviously wanted a holiday.

Once the multiple pots and pans she'd used were washed up and hidden back where they belonged, she pulled a blanket off the couch and slipped onto the deck. Tessa wiggled one of the lounge chairs into a position where she could curl up in the sunshine to wait until Mark returned. For some reason, it was far more important to see him drive up than to work on anything else.

Well, at least with the fast-tracking, it wasn't like taking a lazy day would put the entire project in jeopardy.

Somehow it happened again. She fell asleep, only waking when Mark laid a hand on her shoulder.

"Hey."

He smiled. "Hey, yourself. You want to come inside for some supper?"

Supper? "How did it get to be so late?"

He wiggled his arms under her and lifted, blanket and all. "Well, there's this big ball that we live on called the earth, and it slowly turns in outer space..."

Tessa poked him in the shoulder. "Silly."

He nudged their noses together before lowering her feet to the ground, supporting her until she found her balance.

She giggled. "That was kind of cute."

Mark paused. "What?"

"The careful and tender bit. I'm a cat. You could drop me and I'll still land on my feet." She straightened quickly and kissed his cheek. "Thank you, anyway."

He stared at her for a moment before taking a deep breath and changing the topic. "Something smells incredible in here."

"Oh, that's dinner. Just a minute." She bounced over to the Crock-Pot and popped open the lid. When a rush of amazing scents hit her, she wanted to shout for joy.

Mark stepped behind her. "I thought you couldn't cook."

"I can't. I bet it smells better than it tastes. Something's bound to leap out of nowhere and kill us both." She dipped the spoon into the stew to brave a try.

Mark caught her wrist and guided the scoop toward his own mouth.

Oh dear. "Don't. What if I poison you?"

He blew on the steaming concoction. "I think we'll be okay."

She was tempted to cover her eyes as he closed his lips around the serving.

Mark stood and chewed carefully. She held her breath, waiting for something terrible to happen. He seemed fine so far, a happy hum emitting from his direction.

Then he opened his eyes wide and blinked, right before he fell to the floor.

"Oh, my God, *Mark*." Tessa dropped to her knees at his side, reaching to check if he was choking. If she had killed him, she'd never forgive herself.

Only he rolled, and she was trapped, his teasing smile back in place as he pressed her under him. "Hmm, delicious."

"You scared me." She smacked her fist against his chest. She was going to kill him for real this time.

He leaned down and kissed her. "Sorry. How can I make it up to you?"

Tessa wrapped her legs around him and pulled his lips back to hers, kissing him madly. All her sleepiness had vanished, replaced by a whole lot of other things.

Including a deep rumbling noise that escaped her tummy. Drat—how sexy. A true sign of having missed lunch.

Mark laughed against her lips. "Good thing you made supper, and it's a tasty one."

"We're not done," Tessa warned.

His soft caress along her arm soothed her cat as they found their feet. "Did you have a good day?" he asked, grabbing them bowls and utensils.

She moved the stew to the table, shocked she'd managed to cook something edible. "I had a lazy day."

"Those can be good." Mark breathed deeply as he leaned over the food she'd scooped for him. "Wait until mid-January. We'll have lots of lazy days when the sun goes down early, and it's too cold to do much outside."

Tessa shivered. "Firewood. Lots and lots of firewood stockpiled, right?"

"Of course."

Dinner passed comfortably, her satisfaction rising at every sound of enjoyment Mark made. Suzy-homemaker she wasn't, but feeding him? Whoa, she'd never imagined how gratifying that could be.

Or how erotic. Mark scooped up a spoonful and scarfed it down happily, a tiny smudge of gravy clinging to the corner of his mouth. Tessa reached out without thinking and touched her finger to the spot, cleaning it away.

He caught her wrist, holding her in place until her gaze met his. Then slowly, deliberately, he licked her finger clean.

She swallowed, hard. A buzz shot from where his tongue contacted her through her body all the way until she swore he had licked her clit.

Oh boy.

Where was this leading? They'd played around a couple days ago, but with her strange case of the sleepies, he'd been left hanging for far too long. She wouldn't mind a little more action, either, even if it was far too soon to be committing to anything like being *one true loves* yet.

He released her hand abruptly, refocusing his attention on scraping the remaining bits of food from his bowl.

Tessa hesitated, not quite sure what his withdrawal meant. "Mark? Did I do something wrong?"

"You've done nothing but be yourself, and it's killing me." He lifted his eyes again. "I want you."

Instant shiver—full-body, all-out physical response from head to toe. "I'm good with that."

"Only, I don't want just part of you." He stared past her shoulder, his gaze unblinking as he continued. "You're my mate, and my wolf thinks I'm nuts, but until you're ready to accept me completely, I can't... I thought I could, but I can't make love without going too far."

Her blood raced so hard a blackout seemed possible. "Too far?"

"Marking you. Mating you." He pushed away from the table, opening space between them. "I know I said we could fool around, but I wasn't aware how much being mates would get to me. Maybe if I were a stronger wolf I could handle it. Maybe if you weren't right here—but don't suggest you go anywhere else, because that would only be worse."

Her mouth had gone dry. "You don't want me around, but you don't want me to leave?"

Mark rubbed his forehead. "I'm saying this all wrong, and I'm sorry. I'm trying desperately to give you what you asked for, which is time for us to fall in love. So we're going to have to find ways to spend time together that doesn't involve getting hot and heavy."

Something twisted inside, and it wasn't just her libido complaining. "Oh. Okay. That makes sense."

Only having made him uncomfortable made *her* uncomfortable, and a change of mental game plan for the evening, well, sucked.

While playing Parcheesi or working on a puzzle wasn't what she wanted, she had to respect his honesty. "Thank you for telling me."

"Yeah." He smiled wryly. "Want to go for a run?"

Wednesday

Tessa had deliberately set the alarm to make sure she'd get up in time. When it went off, though, she rolled over, on the verge of falling asleep again as Mark's scent lingering on the sheets made happy little hormones dance in her veins.

At least until she remembered the reason she could smell him had nothing to do with wild romps. It was his bed, ergo, it smelt like him. No late-night orgasms, screaming out in pleasure or even basic cuddling had brought them together.

She forced herself to crawl out from under the covers, wondering what on earth was causing her to be so sleepy these days. Only, it wasn't like exhaustion-tiredness. More as if she was too relaxed to want to bounce from task to task in her usual way.

The sounds of banging led her to the main floor where she found Mark swinging a hammer. Shirtless, his muscles flexing as he moved efficiently again and again, a light sheen of sweat slicking him up.

She clung to the raw wood two-by-four at the entrance to the room to stop from bounding in and jumping him, literally and otherwise.

Instead, Tessa cleared her throat. "Want some breakfast?"

He paused, lifting his head to flash her a wonderful smile that made her heart lift. "Good morning. Breakfast would be super. Hey, I picked up a new coffeemaker—one of those just add water ones. Give it a try. There's a whole box of the decaf thingies it uses on the counter."

"Thank you." She shuffled awkwardly before turning

away. Coffee, breakfast. Then, damn it, she was going to muster up the energy to help hammer boards.

On the second floor one of her sticky notes caught her eye, and she moved in closer to discover he'd written a comment below her suggestion for lighting.

Excellent idea. That will highlight the seating in this area. Well done.

Tessa stared for a moment before wandering the entire floor and reading the comments he'd added to each and every one of her notes. She carried this warm glow with her as she forced herself to keep moving into the day.

Thursday

MARK BUILT FIVE WALLS, three door casements, a couple of bathroom subfloors and roughed in the plumbing for the family guest bathrooms.

In the afternoon he split a cord of wood and stacked it in the woodshed.

Every time he rounded a corner in the paddlewheel and spotted Tessa hard at work on the to-do list they'd put together at breakfast, his need for her flared again, and every time he somehow managed to turn away.

Lying down for the night on the single bed in his Gramps' room was a special kind of torture, knowing she was there, right on the other side of the wall.

Being noble sucked.

Friday

Mark finished the framing on what should have taken at least three weeks, and started on the wiring.

Tessa read through four different manuals regarding cooking for groups, planned sample menus for the B&B, took a nap, put together a couple of different promotional brochures, washed all the sheets and linens, took another nap, scrubbed and polished all the windows including the ones way up high that required her to balance on the top platform of the stepladder.

The email announcing her best friend would be back in town the next morning was the only thing that stopped her from going nuts.

Mark being noble? Sucked.

8

They stepped through the doors of the pack house, Mark a little wary about the upcoming meet-and-greet. Tessa held his arm, staying right beside him. The fact she was touching him, sticking close to his side made it easier.

I love my pack. I trust my pack.

He repeated the words mentally as loudly as he could to drown out the internal voice that whispered taking his unmarked mate—his beautiful, impulsive and sexy mate—into a place with a lot of shifter males was a bad idea.

The issue of her being a cat was high on the list as well, but his wolf was far more concerned about the other problem, go figure.

Tessa squealed with excitement, jiggling on the spot as her arm shot into the air, and she waved frantically. "Keri. There she is. Woohoo."

A rush of relief struck at her enthusiasm—it was the first time in the past couple days that Mark could say Tessa had acted her normal energetic self. His mate was gone like the summer, vanishing between one blink and the next. Keri raced to meet her as well, the two of them tangling together in a huge hug as Keri's mate, Jared, looked on with amusement.

Mark crossed the distance more sedately, but in time to hear the start of the conversation as the two friends curled up on the nearest couch and began catching up.

Jared stood behind them, leaning his hip on the couch. He poked Mark in the arm. "Well, fancy this. Keri told me everything, by the way. You and Tessa, mates, the cat thing."

Drat. "Yeah."

"You need anything, let me know." Jared grinned. "Of course, now I have to wonder what would have happened if you'd made it to the cruise ship on time in July. It would have been you going crazy the entire trip."

Although on the ship they wouldn't have been under each other's feet. "I'm sure it turned out for the best. You and Keri might not have met otherwise."

"It'll all work out in the end." Jared patted him on the back. "Come on, let's grab the girls a drink."

Jared's unexpected echo of TJ's earlier words, the phrase Mark had taken as a mantra, helped calm the wolf inside. Mark leaned over the couch first, putting his lips close to Tessa's ear for a moment as she talked with her best friend. "Sorry to interrupt. What do you want to drink, hot or cold?"

"Cold, please, but no—"

"No caffeine. I got it."

Keri snorted. "He's already got your number."

Tessa stuck out her tongue.

The easy banter should have relaxed him, but Mark was too on edge to let his fears go. He squeezed her shoulder. "We'll be right back. Stay with Keri."

Tessa blinked at him, a question in her eyes, but she didn't argue. "Umm, sure."

He pulled himself away. Each step farther from Tessa felt forced. Painful.

"You're cringing," Jared pointed out.

"I can't help it." Mark looked around the room, eyeing all the lone wolves. Whispered conversations had already started in pockets. He swung his gaze between the two groups that seemed the greatest danger—the most interested in Tessa or the most disgusted to see a cat in their midst. "Everything in me wants to lock her up and hide her away until I know she's officially mine."

"That's going to go over like a ton of bricks, from what Keri said about her friend."

"Yeah, she's...definitely not a wolf." Mark caught the eye of the pack Alpha, and nodded politely. Keil winked in response then turned his attention to the room, and Mark relaxed a little.

If something did start up, he would defend his mate, but with the Alpha obviously on his side, the rest of the pack should think twice about misbehaving.

Jared chuckled softly. "Don't try to play any Poker tonight. Your game face is crap."

"If the shoe was on the other foot, you'd be a nutcase as well." Mark motioned at the pack member working behind the bar. "Two waters with lemon."

"I'd be a total nutcase," Jared agreed. "And drinking something stronger than water."

"Not until I know I don't have to fight." Mark turned to wait, keeping a direct line of sight open to the couch where their women chatted.

"Good point." Jared coughed lightly. "Not that I think you'll need it, but in case? I've got your back, okay?"

Nice. Up to now he and Jared hadn't been close friends, just fellow pack mates and occasional drinking companions, but with their partners being bosom buddies, chances were high the four of them would be seeing a lot of each other.

He glanced over at the other wolf and held out his hand. "Thanks. Appreciate it very much."

Jared accepted his handshake. "You're okay. And since Keri's already talking about all the barbeques and stuff she's going to invite you guys to, you may as well know, with your reputation in the kitchen? You're cooking."

"With your pocketbook? You're buying the steaks."

His new pal laughed. "Deal."

Mark twisted back to check on Tessa, shocked to discover he couldn't see her. One of the single ladies of the pack had stepped between them. The tall woman flashed him a sultry smile as she trailed her fingers down his shirt buttons.

"Mark. Haven't seen you in a few days. Nice you could join us."

"Linda." He caught her wrist to stop her wandering hands from going any lower. A week ago he would have welcomed her exploration. Today, her touch made his skin crawl. "What're you doing?"

She took a deep breath, moving in close enough her hips bumped his, the full swells of her breasts pressing his chest. "Saying hello. You know, you don't need to go slumming."

His wolf snarled at the insult to Tessa. Mark would have pushed Linda away, but he never got a chance.

Tessa was there, slipping between them, her warm backside rubbing his groin. She crossed her arms and used him as a backrest. "Hands off. He's mine."

The thrill her words gave him didn't change the fact

everyone in the pack house was now paying attention, from leadership down to the lowest-ranked wolf.

Mark rubbed Tessa's arms gently. "I got this."

Linda didn't back off. Instead, she raised a brow. "What do you mean, he's yours?" She pressed in closer and sniffed. "I smell eligible wolf."

There were more bodies surrounding them now, and Mark attempted to put Tessa behind him.

She was having none of it. She got right in Linda's face. "Maybe your sniffer is broken."

The other woman shrugged, reached past both of them and picked up a glass off the counter. She lifted it over Tessa's head and tipped it over, soaking her with the contents.

Satisfaction poured from Linda as she tossed the glass aside and cockily crossed her arms. "Nope, my sniffer's working just fine. Now I smell wet cat."

He wanted to snap at Linda, but across the circle, his Alpha shook her head. Robyn and Keil stood at attention— well aware of what was going down. Mark fought for control, but obeyed as Robyn put a finger to her lips, telling him to keep his mouth shut.

If he'd thought not getting to be with Tessa intimately was the worst possible situation he'd experienced in his life, he'd been wrong.

Not defending his mate was by far the hardest thing he'd ever had to do.

THE UNEXPECTED COLD water made her shirt cling to her, a soft *drip, drip, drip* falling from her hair to the floor. The entire room had gone silent as Tessa analyzed the situation.

She was no dummy. Tension had been high since the moment they'd walked in. Even as she'd enjoyed chatting with her BFF, she'd been aware of the discussion going down around the room.

She'd spotted the trouble-making woman well ahead of the attack, and planned her response. The ice water had been unexpected, but she wasn't about to melt.

Tessa had even caught the little gesture by the Alpha—a lovely woman who had the smarts to deal with an unruly bunch of wolves on a regular basis, not to mention the big galoot of a mate at her side.

There had to be a reason Robyn wanted this battle to be Tessa's.

Which was why she mentally considered options rapidly and discarded her first impulses. A straight-out physical confrontation wouldn't prove anything. If she wanted to be accepted by these people, if she was going to not only run a business but mate with one of their own, she couldn't begin by alienating them.

But she couldn't be seen as weak, either.

So she went with the least likely to be expected option. She let loose an enormous, dramatic sigh. "You're right. Wolves' sniffers are a lot more efficient than cats'."

Linda angled her head and gloated.

Tessa reached out and caught the woman by the throat. "He's still mine."

Her sudden move surprised them all, and a low grumble rolled through the crowd. "You haven't marked and mated each other," someone called out, hiding in the background.

Good point. Tessa let go of Linda's neck, patting her cheek before nodding. "True, although in most of the world, a little spit and being someone's chew toy do not make a relationship. But just so there's no doubt. Yo, Keri?"

Her friend pushed into the circle. "Yes?"

"Markers. Please."

Keri pulled her ever-present backpack off her shoulder and dug into the depths. "Any particular colour?"

"Nope." Although bright pink would be fun. Tessa maintained eye contact with the woman who'd started the trouble, hoping that sheer curiosity should stop anyone else from jumping in and starting a rumble.

The asked-for marker flew across the room. Tessa caught it in midair then snapped around to face Mark. He flicked a glance at her before focusing on his pack mates, watching for danger. "I hope you know what you're doing," he muttered.

She grabbed hold of his shirt and tore it apart, buttons clattering to the floor. She hummed happily at the broad expanse of muscles her actions revealed. "Trust me."

Then she put the tip of the marker to his skin and wrote *Property of Tessa Williams* in two-inch-high block letters.

"Dark blue looks good on you. Brings out the colour of your eyes." She laid a hand on his chest, tapping her fingers over where his heart raced. "There, you think that's sufficient for now?"

Mark glanced down. "Permanent marker?"

She peeked at the label. "Yup."

"You should be good for a few weeks if I promise not to rub it off."

Tessa stroked the exposed skin under her hands. "Are they going away?" she whispered.

His gaze darted over her shoulders then back to her face. "Everyone but Keri seems to be real busy all of a sudden. I think we're safe."

"Good." She went to close his shirt and cursed softly. "Sorry about that. You seem to have lost some buttons."

He shrugged out of the material altogether. "I'll just go without for a while. Make sure everyone sees your message." He caught her by the chin and smiled. "You *are* unpredictable."

"I'm nice too. I considered writing it on your forehead." She cuddled against his warmth, strangely happy at the unusual twist to the evening.

"Well done." The deep voice brought her around to see the pack Alphas, Keil and Robyn, standing a few feet away.

Mark straightened up and dipped his head politely. "Sorry for the commotion."

"Not your fault." Keil eyed her, and Tessa coughed lightly.

Yeah, okay totally her responsibility. "Hi."

The head of the Granite Lake pack looked very serious for a moment until his mate elbowed him in the side, and he broke out laughing. "Right. Robyn wants me to let you know we'd like to have you two over for dinner later this week."

Sweet. "We'd love to." Tessa snuck her fingers into Mark's. "Can we bring anything?"

Keil turned to his mate, moving his hands in sign language. Tessa watched in fascination as Robyn responded. It was one of the most beautiful things she'd ever seen. She immediately put *learn sign language* on her bucket list.

Keil faced them again. "If you'd like to bring dessert, that would be great. I'll call later to set the date."

Mark leant over to whisper in her ear. "I'll cook."

"Hush, your Alphas are listening. Be polite."

Robyn hadn't stopped grinning, only now she reached out to offer her hand. Tessa accepted it happily, pleased at the gesture.

The Alphas excused themselves, wandering through the pack house and visiting with people, making sure everything went back to normal. Tensions seemed to have faded after Tessa's little display, and she tucked herself against Mark's side and hauled him back to the area they'd been sitting originally.

Really, it had been a pretty good evening, except for the wetness clinging to her body.

Keri shook her head. "Troublemaker."

"Hey, it wasn't me." Tessa crossed her legs under her and relaxed on the couch. Mark had draped his arm along the back of the headrest, enclosing her in his embrace without touching her. It was cozy and warm, and she felt like purring—it was the closest she'd been to being in his arms in days. "Well, it wasn't *just* me. It had to happen, and it might not be the last time someone objects to having a cat around. We'll deal with it."

Jared stared at the pen markings. "What I don't get, and excuse me, I'm just a simple wolf... Why?"

"Why, what?"

He pointed. "Why are you claiming him without claiming him? I mean if you don't want Mark as a mate, I can understand that. I bet you can find someone better." He winked to show he was mostly teasing.

Mark growled. "You're not helping."

She wasn't sure herself. "Mark says we're mates. You think he's lying?"

Utter shock at the suggestion flashed in both their faces.

"Um, why would he lie about something like that?" Keri frowned. "I don't know that a wolf *could* lie about something like that."

"Right. So...once we get to know each other and a little more time passes, I figure he's got a good chance at being the one for me. I'm not letting anyone else drool on him."

Keri nodded slowly, then shot to her feet. "Come on, I need to talk to you."

In a total change of situation, this time it was Tessa being dragged across the floor to the front doors.

The guys rose, but Keri waved them off. "Alone. Give us a minute."

The pack was getting some entertainment tonight. Tessa waved at the cluster of women where Linda had retreated. Two seconds later she was out the door and down the stairs, being backed against the outside railing by her best friend.

Keri glared at her. "Okay, blunt-speaking time. Are you out of your damn feline mind?"

What in the world? "No more than usual. What's wrong?"

"*You're* what's wrong. I can't believe you lived next to wolves your entire life and you're acting like this." Keri paused and dragged her hand through her hair. "I mean, okay—you were brilliant with the marker thing. And yes, I vaguely see your point in terms of wanting to be in love before you make it official..."

There was an unspoken *but* written all over the silence that fell as Keri's words faded away.

"*What?*"

Her best friend shook her head. "Mark said you're mates. You kind of, mostly, believe him. You just claimed him...and now what?"

"And now we're going to turn the paddle wheeler into a B&B?"

Keri poked her in the shoulder. "No. You're going to be nice to the guy and give him a break."

She still didn't get it. "Nope, you lost me."

Keri dragged her closer. "When we were on the cruise ship, and I'd sniffed out Jared? I swear it was seven kinds of hell waiting until we figured out what was wrong and finally mated. You just told me about all the things Mark's been doing around the B&B. All the fast-tracking and hard work he's been putting in to make you happy... What the *hell* are you waiting for? Him to spout poetry and recite some specific lines you think you need to hear?"

"Is it wrong to want romance? To want fine gestures and romantic words? 'I would die for you'—all that kind of thing."

Her best friend laughed. "Oh, Tessa, you're getting romance in the movies mixed up with the real romance of life. Not everyone does things the same way, right? Not everyone is going to say *I love you* the same way."

Tessa clung to her ideals, even as they seemed to whither a little. "But Romeo and Juliet—"

Keri's expression darkened, and Tessa jerked to a stop before she got bitten.

"If ever there were a couple of sickies... How does that story end, Tessa? With partners who listen to each other? Who grow old together? That's not romance, it's nothing but selfish, sorry people screwing up big time."

Her friend's admonishment was enough to make Tessa ashamed. "I've been so focused on the changes around the place, and all the plans I came to Haines to accomplish, I didn't think."

Keri rolled her eyes. "Stop with the excuses. And I'm not telling you that you need to simply accept him."

"Aren't you?"

Her friend eyed her, changing her tone to *whatever*-ish. "Okay. Fine. So you're saying you don't feel closer to him now than before you met him? As far as you're concerned it could be Linda he's building things for. And other than you don't want leftovers, it wouldn't really bother you if she was the one curled up in his lap, running her fingers over his body—"

"Hey." A hot flush of anger slid over her at the thought. "Now you're getting nasty."

"I'm being honest."

Tessa froze, the seriousness of her friend's expression making her listen, not just to the words, but to the lingering aftershocks of annoyance conjured from imagining Mark with anyone but her.

Keri lowered her voice. Slowed her tirade. "I realize as a wolf I can't truly understand where you're coming from. What's built into me doesn't compute when I hear you talking about what you need. I hear you say you want to wait for the forever part of the deal, wait until the sunset is just right or something. It makes no sense."

If her friend couldn't understand, what was Mark feeling?

Keri caught hold of Tessa's arms and held her tight. "Maybe that sounds as if I'm putting down your choices, and I don't mean to. You're a good friend, Tessa, and a good, *good* person. What you're doing isn't good, though. You're being mean to that wonderful man, because while wanting you to be his mate *right here and right now* might not be the cat way, he's not a cat. And you can only push the wolf so hard before he'll break."

9

Tessa had been strangely quiet since she and Keri returned to the pack house. She curled under his arm again, but this time all the fidgeting seemed to have drained from her.

Mark stroked her arm gently, worried. "Are you okay? What did Keri say to you?"

"Nothing but the truth." She blinked hard, and his heart skipped a beat.

"Are you crying?" He touched her cheek. "Don't be sad. There's nothing we can't face together, okay?"

That only seemed to make her sniff harder. "Can we go home?"

The words snuck out slowly.

"Of course." He brought her to her feet. They made their goodbyes to their friends, Mark resisting the urge to give Keri a dirty look for whatever it was she'd done to upset Tessa.

The short ride home passed in silence. The exterior lights were on at the house, the upper floor sparkling with the new fixtures she'd chosen and he'd rushed to install.

He pointed them out to her. "You picked the perfect ones. I love how they look."

Tessa smiled, but it never reached her eyes. She tugged him to a stop before they hit the door. "Wait. I need to...look around."

This night got more and more confusing. "Of course."

She caught his fingers in hers and refused to let him go. The feel of her skin under his hand—he'd never got the concept of pleasure/pain before, but being with her without being *with* her was teaching him fast.

There didn't seem to be anywhere specific she wanted to go. They shot past the full wood shed, through the freshly painted paddlewheel blades that she'd mentioned would look great in dark green, around the outside where he'd begun to widen the front walkway.

Tessa brought him inside and paced through the rooms that were ready and waiting for the drywall that was on order—he'd run out of things to build. While waiting for supplies, he'd switched to making furniture.

She trailed her fingers over the smoothly sanded surface of a bedpost, still not talking. Not explaining what was wrong.

His wolf was ready to burst free when she finally smiled. A real smile. "Come upstairs, I have something to show you."

The beast inside calmed enough he could take the stairs at her side without panicking. But when she stopped in the kitchen of all places, he couldn't hold it in any longer.

"Tessa, what the heck is wrong? What did Keri say?"

She poked at the new coffeemaker on the island countertop. "Keri told me to open my eyes and stop being a fool."

One more tug, and she had him in the large open space

where the giant table for the group dinners would sit. When she would have brought him to the floor, he hesitated.

"Tessa, this isn't a good idea." If he got down with her, she might not get up for the rest of the night. "I'll just go—"

"Stay," she ordered. "I need to tell you something important."

He knelt, keeping a bit of distance between them.

She eyed the space, and sighed unhappily.

His heart ached, but he didn't break. Not yet. Not until she lifted her gaze to meet his, and her eyes were full of unshed tears.

Mark moved without thinking, scooping her up and cradling her in his lap, holding her head to his shoulder and rocking her. The connection between their bodies heated like a branding iron, but somewhere he'd find the power to give her what she needed without claiming her.

Her fingers brushed his cheek. "You've been saying it all along, haven't you?"

He paused, partly because her touch was driving electric pulses through his entire system, and partly because he wasn't sure what she meant.

She wiggled upright and held his face in both her hands. "You've been saying it all along and I wasn't listening. That's what Keri smacked me over the head with —that I'm a cat and you're a wolf. It wasn't a stupid comment that my brother made not very long ago."

"Tony?" Had she been chatting with her family? "That reminds me. I wanted to suggest you invite everyone over for a visit. Your mom, dad, Tony. Whenever works for them. We'll have room—"

Her mouth covered his, stopping his rush of words and, holy moly, he really was going to die now. Because after a few days without tasting her, there was no way he'd be able to convince his wolf to stop. The buzz of chemicals turned him inside out, *longing* far too soft of a word for what he felt.

Her lips caressed delicately though, and his fingers trembled on her hips as he fought for control.

A slick of tongues together. The shaking increased to include his arms.

When she buried her hands in his hair and leaned back, pulling him over her, he was torn between stripping them naked and worrying about her getting hurt on the hard wood floor.

Her entire body softened as they kissed, his groin so tight to hers he was afraid he might spontaneously erupt. Mark rolled, putting her on top, protecting her from the cold and the unpadded surface.

His gums ached with the urge to mark her, to take her, to possess her. But while she was kissing him, at least he wasn't doing anything crazy-like.

Tessa planted her palms to his chest and pushed herself upright, straddling his hips and pinning him in place. Well, as much as a lightweight like her could keep him trapped.

She calmed her breathing, and that beautiful smile he'd fallen in love with returned to brighten her face. "Do you even know you're doing it?"

"That I'm lying on the floor trying not to ravish you? Oh, I know, sweetheart. I know."

She shook her head. "I mention I'm worried about the cold winter—you fill the shed with a two-year supply of wood. I try to break your coffeemaker; you get me a different one. You've worked and worked and listened to every single thing I've said, and I'm so ashamed of myself..."

He curled himself upright, sexual tension temporarily

forgotten in an attempt to reassure her. "Hey, stop that. You haven't done anything wrong."

Tessa tilted her head to the side. "Maybe not if you were a cat, but you're a wolf. And even if you were a cat, I'm guilty of one terrible thing. I haven't been listening. Not like you have. Can you forgive me?"

Mark was lost, but... "Sure. I forgive you. But are you going to tell me what specifically I'm forgiving you for?"

She stroked his chest lightly. "I had my own agenda when I came out here, and that's not wrong. It's good for me to have goals, and even though we're mates, I'm not going to give up thinking things through and making plans."

"I wouldn't want you to," he insisted.

She nodded. "I know, yet that's why I'm sorry. I had an idea of what 'being in love' looked like, and when you didn't do *those* things, I figured we had to wait. I wasn't listening to what you were really saying."

His brain had focused in on one part of her confession. "You figured we had to wait. Does that mean...we don't have to any longer?"

Tessa paused. "Do you love me?"

"Of course I do." His heart raced. "I mean, I'll fall in love with you more as time goes past, but right now I can still say honestly that I love you."

"You love me because we're mates..."

Mark laughed. "You're still hung up on that, aren't you? I know it's not a cat way. But, Tessa, I love you because you're *you*. That's why we're mates in the first place. I wouldn't have this draw inside toward a random stranger who wasn't perfect for me. Who wouldn't complement my talents, who couldn't enjoy the things I enjoy. It's not like a shortcut to happiness because we need to work at it, but we're *right* together. That's what being mates means."

Enough. He stood and carried her into the bedroom. This time he dropped her—actually, he lofted her toward the bed.

Tessa twisted with a feline grace and landed on all fours, the most incredible smile beaming back at him. "Like I said, you listen all the time."

~

THIS INCREDIBLE MIXTURE of sorrow and delight filled her.

She'd screwed up, badly, but he wasn't going to hold it against her. That much she knew without the slightest doubt.

Tessa sat back on her heels. Stared at him as he waited patiently, as usual. "Remember I told you I don't feel successful at times?"

He nodded.

"That doesn't change the facts. I'm good at what I do. I have the skills, I have the drive and the enthusiasm, and I work and make things happen."

There was a distance between them, but hope lit his eyes—just a flutter of it crossing his face. "Feelings and reality aren't always the same thing?"

"No." There was so much she wasn't certain about, only she'd been an idiot to ignore the specific truths in this situation. "Mark, you're a wolf."

His face twisted as he attempted to hide his laughter. "Umm, yes. You said that already."

"I might need to say it a few more times, just to get it to sink into my thick cat skull. You're a wolf, *and* you love me. We're mates, and that's not going to change for you."

His dark eyes sparkled. "Nope. Well, it'll get stronger—the being-in-love-with-you part."

This time his assurance sent a thrill through her, and that was the final nudge she needed to move forward. Now how to say this without sounding like a diva, a freak or bitch? The last thing she wanted was to remove the happiness blooming on his face.

She squared her shoulders and went for honest. "I'm stealing your line—it's going to get stronger for me too. The falling-in-love-with-you part."

Mark sucked in a breath.

She hurried on before he could interrupt. "Since I'm a cat and all?—my feelings don't work like yours. I mean, we met barely a week ago, so me being in love with you doesn't make sense. But that doesn't mean I can't make the proper choice right now."

Two shuffles put her at the edge of the bed where she caught hold of his belt buckle in one hand and dragged him toward her. His uneasy smile had grown stronger...like the love between them would grow. She was sure of it now.

"I *choose* to be your mate, Mark. I choose to accept all the love you've poured out for me, and I'm going to smarten up and start listening to the quiet, hardworking ways you say it. I'm going to let the feelings come whenever they come, but in the meantime?" She stared up and let all the admiration she had for him shine out. All the longings she had as well. "I think you're pretty damn amazing, and I would be honoured to be your mate. I can't wait to fall in love with you as hard as your wolf is already in love with me."

For one terrible, horrible no-good-moment, Mark didn't budge. Tessa considered repeating her confession, but that seemed so—

He pounced.

Tessa squealed as he bore her to the mattress, his weight pressing her down as he found her lips.

When he lifted his head far enough they could both suck for oxygen, all traces of his faint smile were gone, replaced with an enormous grin. "I had to fall in love with a cat."

She could have sworn her cougar preened. *Silly beastie.*

"You're okay with it all?"

He nodded. "You making a choice? Blows my mind. I'm going to make sure you never regret it."

"Cats aren't all bad, you know…" There was just enough room between them. She stripped down to nothing far quicker than even his needy wolf could ask.

His delighted growl filled the air. "Neat trick."

Then it was past time for talking. Time for doing—for giving to the other side of them, and giving to Mark what he'd been so patiently waiting for. Tessa caught him around the neck and pulled him back against her naked body.

She tugged at his clothing as they kissed, all tongues, teeth and lips, their heavy panting echoing through the room.

Mark licked her neck, and Tessa shivered as she protested, "You have too many clothes on."

"The only way I can make it last longer than thirty seconds."

"We can just do it again," she pointed out.

"We will," he promised. "Again, and again, and again. But this first time?"

He slipped down to worship her breasts, and Tessa's satisfaction rose at having seen the light.

He didn't have to know everything about her now. She didn't know everything about herself—she'd assumed she couldn't cook, but she'd managed to learn. If she was changing and growing, then they could change and grow together as mates.

He nibbled just the right way, and the tingles turned into full-body pulses. "You're going to mark me, right?"

"Everywhere. Like you're my own personal chew toy." His teeth went into the side of her breast, and the ensuing shot of sexual pleasure lifted her off the bed.

Mark caught her hips in his hands and locked her in position, trailing his tongue over her stomach until he reached her belly button. Her hipbones. The ticklish crease between her leg and torso. The cold air brushed past everywhere he touched, and she got goose bumps all over her body.

"Hmm, you smell delicious." She shuffled up on her elbows just in time to see him inhale deeply, his expression one of complete contentment.

Tessa held her breath as he slipped a finger through her curls. She bit her lip as he lowered his head. And she lost it all when he snuck out his tongue to taste her.

She collapsed back on the bed, opened her thighs as wide as she could and prepared for the explosion that was sure to come. Each graze of his tongue like a flick of a timer, the old-fashioned ones with little numbers that fell in sequence.

One stroke.

Another, this time from her core to the bundle of aching nerves she wanted him to focus on. Tessa drove her fingers into his hair and attempted to keep him in one spot, but he chuckled evilly and thrust his tongue lower, into her body, humming as he lapped at her sex.

He seemed so occupied it shocked her when another

touch hit. She peered through half-lidded eyes to see what went with the amazing sensation.

He'd spread his palm over her lower belly, his thumb centered over her clit. As he continued to lick, he pressed down, the tight circle focused on her trigger button.

Tessa called out his name as she came, gasping for air as he didn't let up but did it all over again until the pulses from her core and the lack of air from gasping threatened to make her pass out.

Mark lifted up, just enough to strip off his shirt, and the words on his chest made her laugh out loud. "I can't believe you let me write on you like that."

He'd lost his pants and boxers, and crawled beside her in all his naked glory. He caught her hand and pressed it to the thick blue lines. "It's true. I'm yours."

Not yet, he wasn't, but nearly. Tessa's cat preened and fussed, happy from the orgasms, but wanting it all. She reached between them and closed her fingers around him carefully, loving the contrast of hard shaft and soft skin. "No condoms."

He shook his head. "You tell me. As shifters we're good, but..."

"I'm a cat. I can't get pregnant right now." His eyes rolled back as she stroked him, playing with the amount of pressure, the speed.

Mark caught her wrist. "Stop."

Wow. "How do you talk through your teeth like that?"

He grinned and leaned in to kiss her until she tingled all over. He rolled over her, nudging her thighs apart with his knees.

"Look at me," he ordered.

Tessa stared into his eyes as his cock slipped between

her folds. Heat and pressure and something else slid into her, a sensory overload of pleasure. Of belonging.

His.

Together.

Mark buried himself all the way. Tessa lifted her legs around his waist and moaned in delight.

"This. This is only part of it." Mark pulled his hips back so slowly, his cock teasing as it rubbed the perfect places inside. He rocked forward and her breath gasped out, forced by the depths of his possession.

The entire time he took her, he watched. His gaze drifted over her face, her torso. Hungrily memorizing her? Whatever it was, Tessa was on fire. It had never been like this before. Something deeper than physical connection wrapped around her. Drew them together.

Mark kissed her without missing a stroke. Harder drives now, his breath fanning past her cheek. His cock a hard point of pleasure taking her again, and again. Tessa arched up to add to the motion, squeezing her thighs, digging her heels into his ass until the sound of their bodies echoed through the room. Panting breaths, frantic motions.

A blinding rush of desire in her core burst out, pulsing around him and wringing his climax from him. Mark brought his teeth to her neck and bit down and...

There were no fireworks, no twirling lights. It was like being thrown from a massive height yet knowing there was a safety net to catch her. Mark was that net. Mark would always be there to catch her. Free fall, a rush of excitement that made her cat thrill and her human clutch his shoulders and rock.

"That was totally wicked..."

She'd meant to say it out loud, but her ears never heard the words.

Mark stiffened, though, as if she had spoken. His every muscle had gone tight, his teeth buried in her neck like his cock was buried in her sex. He jerked, the final pulses of his release escaping as he groaned.

"Tessa, oh damn, I can't believe it."

She was too bonelessly satisfied to bounce with excitement. *"Whoa...I can hear you in my head."*

Mark licked her. Pressed his lips to the spot that radiated waves indicating something...other...had just happened. *"Mate bond. This is it. You're mine."*

Tessa nuzzled the side of his head until he twisted far enough their lips met. It seemed like the appropriate moment for a kiss. *"I think this means you're* mine. *After all, you are the one who's labeled and all."*

Mark chuckled against her lips. "Semantics."

She shook her head seriously. "No way. To a cat? Ownership is everything. You're *mine.*" Tessa rocked her hips, pleased to discover that another one of the stories she'd heard about wolves and mates wasn't a fable. "Hmm, you're hard again."

"I noticed." Mark sighed wearily. "Guess we'll just have to start all over and try harder."

Tessa laughed before she caught his head in her hands. "I'm thrilled to be yours. And I'm going to love you more as time goes by. If you're okay with that."

His grin alone would have been enough of an answer— she was a quick study, she had figured out listening to what actions said was important.

Still, she couldn't deny that the words he whispered through their mate bond gave her a thrill.

"As you wish..."

10

———

December

Mark nodded at the pack mate who slipped through the open front door. "Upstairs. Third floor. Take the dish to the kitchen, and the tree is in the gathering area."

He stuck his head out the front door for a moment. The north wind howling over the piled-high snow made him even more grateful for the warmth of the house behind him. He raced up the stairs, bursting into the body-filled area of the main entertainment area. The sounds of happy conversation and laughter competed with Christmas carols and the crackle of the fire.

Tessa bounded across the room to his side. She planted a huge kiss on his cheek, her arms circling him so naturally he sighed with contentment.

"Is that everyone you invited?" He glanced around the room. "Looks as if the entire pack is here."

She tilted her head to the side. "Your high exalted ones had other commitments and couldn't make it, but yeah, I think just about everyone else said yes. Nice turnout for our first soirée."

"You've done an incredible job. Thank you for making my pack welcome."

She beamed at him. "They're my pack now too, you know."

And they were. Somehow, she'd managed to bewitch the lot of them. Whether it had something to do with the fact he and Tessa were most definitely mates, or the way she refused to back down from trouble, things had worked out fine. There'd been a few displays of power in the pack house, but through them all Tessa had never lost her sense of humour.

Wolves liked that.

Tessa bumped him again. "Thanks for inviting my brother to come spend Christmas with us—he's having a blast."

She pointed to a corner where the massive blond cougar was draped over a chair, partially hidden from sight by the lady wolves fawning over him. Even more incredibly, there were a half dozen of the pack's single male wolves all gathered around as well, none of whom were threatening to rip Tony apart for poaching.

Mark shook his head in disbelief. "How can he get away with that? I'm surprised no one has offered to find a deep crevasse and drop him into it."

Tessa shrugged. "He's got charm out the ying-yang."

Mark held on to his mate and gazed around contentedly, amazed how much difference a few months could make.

They'd turned the paddle wheeler into not only a B&B ready state, but a home. They'd done it together.

The long table Tessa had drawn for him to make graced

the window-filled area, lights on the balcony sparkling against the darkness of the December night sky. To the right, before the fire, Gramps rocked lazily, ruling supreme over a covey of his cronies.

The kitchen hadn't changed much, except now it was filled with wolves all fussing with food and drinks—the kind of laughter and noise he'd often experienced at the pack house but less often here at home.

At least until Tessa had come along.

He squeezed her tighter to his side, loving that she was there. Where she belonged. Together.

"I need your advice on something." She tugged him toward the kitchen, smiling at random wolves and accepting their teasing good-naturedly. "Come on, Fido, out of my way."

She hip-checked Keri. Gently, though, out of consideration for her best friend's swelling belly.

Keri shook her head and shifted her widening girth to the side. "My mate hears you've been manhandling me again, he's going to give you hell."

Tessa pulled out a tray of cookies and offered Keri one. "That's an idle threat, and you know it. Your mate loves me. All the Granite Lake wolfies love their kitty mascot."

Keri picked up a cookie and eyed it suspiciously. "Umm, yeah. Fine, you're right. You've managed to brainwash everyone else into believing you're the greatest thing since—"

"Flea collars?"

Mark stifled his amusement, at least until Keri lifted a cookie his direction, her one brow raised high. "Did you see what your mate baked for Christmas?"

The sweet treat was shaped like a bone.

Tessa lowered the tray, her grin firmly in place.

"They're peanut butter with extra crunch. Good for your molars."

Mark glanced down at the island, checking it out more thoroughly. "What in the hell?"

All the serving bowls were dog dishes.

He shook his head. At some point his mate was going to push too hard. But then again, the pack seemed to enjoy trying to one-up her.

"Hey, Tessa," TJ called from the living area. "I brought you a decoration."

He held up a handful of sparkling tinsel and shook it in the air.

Tessa leapt up and raced across the room, pulling to a stop just shy of his pack mate. She twisted her fingers behind her back. "I hope you plan on giving that to me, or you're just a big tease."

TJ laughed and handed over half, moving to the tree at her side and helping drape the shimmering strands.

Mark watched contentedly as his mate worked the room, chatting with some, teasing others. Even the tension between Linda and Tessa had vanished during some kind of Girls Night Out ritual Tessa had started that involved way too much alcohol, laughter and dirty jokes.

Or so he'd been told. He'd never actually witnessed a GNO, since he was banished from the B&B on those nights.

Her gaze caught his, and even though they were across the room from each other, it was as if they were right there. Connected. One.

"Having fun, sweetheart?" Mark asked.

She didn't move from where she stood beside his Gramps. *"As much fun as a cat in a hen house."*

He sent her a mental snort. "You mean a cat in a kennel, don't you?"

She grinned. "Wait until Pam opens her gift—I bought her a really cool dog collar."

Mark frowned. *"But Pam's human...oh."* He glanced at TJ and laughed out loud. One thing for certain, Tessa knew how to liven up a celebration.

~

THE FIRE WAS DOWN to glowing embers. Wrapping-paper scraps littered the floor and poked out from under the couch. Tessa leaned against Mark's chest and sighed happily. "That was an awesome party, if I do say so myself."

Her mate did nothing but hum in response, so she wiggled around to face him.

Mark cracked one eye open. "Yes, awesome. Now we get to move into lazy-relaxing season, correct?"

She mock gasped. "Lazy? You mean you don't feel like doing more renovations?"

He groaned even as he pulled her alongside his body and nestled her in comfortably. "We're done, sweetheart. The place is ready for the spring. You're already getting bookings, the furniture is complete. We've got months before the first people will show up. Definitely time to hit relaxing mode."

Tessa played with his buttons. "I guess so. If you insist."

A snort of laughter escaped him. "How about we go back to those days when you slept like twelve hours straight? I could use a few of those."

"You know that's not going to happen." Tessa resisted poking him. "And that's not nice, bringing that up. I didn't know my cat was causing it."

He lifted her chin and kissed her slowly, taking his time

like he was dead serious about them switching into slow motion.

She didn't fight it. He was too good a kisser, and that lovely distraction made her far too happy to complain. *"I love you."*

Mark rumbled with happiness at her words.

The fact she could say it with complete honesty was a little bit of heaven. He never seemed to get tired of her repeating it, either.

She brushed her lips over his cheek and said it out loud, just for emphasis. "I love you inside and out. I love you, I lov—"

He crushed his mouth over hers, and this time there was nothing slow about it.

When they finally came up for air, they'd lost their clothing.

Strange.

Tessa pressed her naked body to his, loving how the heat of the fire and the rosy-red haze blanketed them as they lay on the thick rug.

They'd been mates for months now, and the connection simply got better and better. Thank goodness for friends who wouldn't shut up, and mates who wouldn't give up.

Mark stroked her naked shoulder, seemingly as fascinated by the firelight as she had been. "Yip, your cat knew all along we were meant to be together. All that nesting and snoozing was her trying to convince your human side to slow down and accept what was meant to be. Have I mentioned lately how much I like your cat?"

Tessa didn't fight the urge. She shifted, right there in his arms, meaning he had a whole lot of cougar pressed up against him.

He jolted for a second. "Very funny."

"Well, you said you liked my cat..."

He didn't struggle as she licked him once, a full-face-wash type of grooming move that satisfied something deep inside her cat nature. Then while he was still laughing, she shifted back and proceeded to satisfy the human sides for both of them.

Mates. Who knew they could be so much fun?

EPILOGUE

The following June

ark pulled into one of the *Reserved for Owner* parking stalls, chuckling as he noticed that once again there'd been an additional comment added to his sign.

His *kitten with a sense of humour* had continued to put her markers to good use since they'd finished the parking area. This time instead of something like "No Bears Allowed", or "*Woof, Woof, Woof*" with a little star following indicating that meant *Mark's place*, today Tessa had gone straight to the point.

All capital letters that boldly proclaimed:

GOOD BOY

They'd made a deliberate decision to not book the B&B full every day of the season. Tessa had suggested leaving gaps, and like all the suggestions his mate made, Mark was happy to go along with her. The calendar showed a solid line blocked off through a week in June and one in September, and while they'd lose revenue, Tessa had pointed out that a week to take a breath and spend quality time together was important.

The fact she was able to suggest taking a breather was a miracle all in itself.

But the extra cars in the parking lot and the volume of noise as he made his way up the stairs warned there wasn't going to be *alone* quality time, at least not for a while. Something special had obviously come up after he'd kissed her goodbye four hours ago so he could go give Jared a hand on the nursery he and Keri expected to fill any day now.

But, as Mark had learned over the past months, *anywhere* was now a party when Tessa was involved.

Along with the voices came the scents, and as he continued his hurried rush forward, Mark began sorting out who he would find crashing his home in the middle of the day. Keri was there, along with most of the other ladies in pack leadership. In a delightful twist it had turned out that Tessa had a flair for learning sign language, and she and Robyn were now thick as thieves.

Although to be truthful, Tessa's interpretations of what Robyn said sometimes left a little to be desired.

So, Tessa had been invaded by the ladies of the pack. He grinned. He loved that his pack loved her, too.

Sure enough, at the top of the stairs Mark was hit by a horde of short people. The half dozen women in the pack had brought their youngsters, and as he climbed over the gate guarding the top landing he was surrounded by munchkins all shouting his name enthusiastically.

Mark dropped to his knees and held out his arms as he cried out in mock alarm. "Oh no, I'm being attacked by wolves."

Giggles ensued as at least seven little people jumped into his arms and onto his back. The Omegas' little boy

Jamie climbed like a cat onto his shoulders then grabbed Mark's ears like reins.

Mark caught hold of the little tyke's wrists to protect himself from being peeled like a banana. "Whoa there, cowboy. Those are attached to me."

"Cookies are ready." The announcement rang across the room, and the squirming horde abandoned Mark for sweeter pastures.

He glanced into the kitchen to discover the pack Omega, Missy grinning at him.

Mark brushed his knees off and made his way to her side. "Thanks for the save."

She held out a pair of cookies. "Sorry about my enthusiastic son," she offered in return.

"Anything special I'm interrupting?" Mark asked.

"Not really." Her bright smile faded slightly. "Oops. Someone's not happy."

They both glanced around the room, Mark focusing in on his mate in seconds flat. She was easy to track down through their connection, and his gaze went instantly to where she was holding court in the corner of the room. A group of three old timers including Gramps were all staring intently at their cards as Tessa and Robyn faced each other down.

Neither of the women were smiling.

Uh-oh. From the death glare on Robyn's face, something was wrong, or something was *really* wrong.

"I'll get this," he told Missy. "Keep the cavalry from interrupting."

He sauntered slowly to keep from drawing attention to the situation while itching to close the distance as quickly as possible. Once he was able to, he laid a hand on Tessa's shoulder and leaned down to nuzzle the side of her neck. "Are you behaving yourself, sweetheart?"

Robyn lifted her hands and signed rapidly—definitely a complaint, and most of which Mark didn't understand.

Tessa interpreted. "She says I'm never going to give you up. Never going to let you down. Never gonna run around or desert you."

Robyn's hands faltered for a second before increasing in speed, as if speaking more intently.

"Never going to make you cry, never gonna say good bye—"

Mark covered Tessa's mouth with his hand, fighting back his laughter. "You did not just rick-roll us."

She blinked innocently. "What I meant is Robyn says I'm being the best little kitty-cat on the face of the planet."

The pack Alpha folded her arms, tilted her head, and glared. Ice in her eyes.

"Or... she might have said she thinks I'm cheating. They look a lot alike, the signs for those two things."

At this, the three gentlemen at the table lifted their eyes off their cards to Mark, and nodded seriously before once again dropping their gazes in submission.

Only Gramps had shared just the hint of a wink before the surging power of a pissed-off Alpha wolf forced his head down.

Mark counted his blessings. One, Robyn wasn't mad at *him*. Two, the fact it was his mate about to be ripped a new one and his wolf was willing to go up against *anyone*, even their Alpha if need be, for her sake.

Those were the only reasons he was strong enough to keep his feet and make a suggestion. "There are hot cookies. Why don't you gentlemen take a break and leave the cards for a while?"

Three empty chairs sprang into existence as Gramps and his two cronies vanished to safer territory near Missy and the warm cookies.

Mark held one of his cookies to Robyn. "This is for you."

Robyn was still glaring, but her nose twitched. She let out a huge sigh before shaking her finger at Tessa and accepting Mark's offering.

"Did you bring a cookie for me?" Tessa asked, all sweetness and light.

Mark settled in the chair beside her, keeping one hand on the back of her neck in case she decided to bolt before they were finished. "Tessa. Forget about the cookies. Why were you cheating?"

She gasped indignantly, propping her hands on her hips.

He gave her another *look*. "If Robyn thinks you're cheating, then you probably are." Mark offered his Alpha an apologetic glance before turning back to his mate. "Not because I trust her more than you, but because she's...*Robyn*."

Tessa snorted, but she nodded.

Mark continued. "But I also know this. I'm sure you're cheating for a very *very* good reason."

His mate let out a huge sigh then turned to Robyn. "He's a meanie. He's going to make me admit what I was doing."

Robyn's brow rose skyward as she signed "damn right."

Tessa glanced over her shoulder before rising from her chair, slipping to the far side of the table, and lowering her voice. She signed along with her softly spoken explanation. "I was cheating, but it's because of this..."

She dipped down out of sight for a moment before rising up and sliding a thick pile of cards across the table top. Aces, kings and queens—far more than usually found in a regular deck of cards stared up at them for a moment before Tessa quickly gathered them together and hid them away.

"Tessa?" Mark couldn't believe his eyes. "Where were those—extra face cards? Who put them there?"

Robyn's lips twitched for a second before she burst out laughing, rose from the table and wrapped Tessa in a huge squishy hug. She stepped away just far enough to rub Tessa's head briefly before signing too rapidly for Mark to follow.

Tessa smiled, pretending to turn a lock on her lips then throwing away the key.

Robyn patted Mark on the shoulder then returned to the main gathering in the kitchen.

Trouble averted, then. Not that Mark really knew what had just happened, and that was pretty par for the course. His life was one giant whirlwind, and he wouldn't have it any other way. But still...

"Tessa? Want to explain?"

She curled herself under his arm and cuddled in against his body, speaking softly. "Gramps was having a bad day, and I was trying to make him smile. None of the guys can shuffle very well, so Robyn and I were taking turns for them, and I was kinda sneaking extra cards into the deck so he'd have better hands."

"You were cheating to give *Gramps* the winning hands?"

"Uh-huh."

"Card sharp. Oh, sweetie, that was nice of you, but not a good idea. What if it made the other players unhappy?" He frowned. "Wait. That also doesn't explain the extra cards tucked away under the table."

Tessa shrugged. "Your gramps has nice friends. Every time they helped gather up the cards, they pulled the extras out and hid them so Robyn wouldn't notice."

His mate was nothing if not thorough when she got in trouble. "So the only person *not* cheating at the table was...Robyn?"

Tessa grinned. "It's okay. She just told me that I'm forgiven as long as I don't do it again—and as long as I'm her partner the next time we play Canasta."

Mark laughed, pressing a kiss to her lips as she curled her arms around him. Then he stood there with his happiness in his arms and looked contentedly around his home. It was filled to the brim with family, friends, pack, and Tessa—his lover, his heart and his soul.

He had it all, with so much more to look forward to.

His mate purred softly in his arms, head resting on his chest. "I love having a pack," she whispered. "But most of all, I love having you as my everything."

It was too perfect to resist. Mark purred back.

~

New York Times Bestselling Author Vivian Arend
brings you a series of light-hearted,
stand-alone novellas, with fated mates and always a
happily-ever-after.

~

Granite Lake Wolves
Wolf Signs
Wolf Flight
Wolf Games
Wolf Tracks
Wolf Line
Wolf Nip

~

ABOUT THE AUTHOR

New York Times and *USA Today* bestselling author Vivian Arend loves to share the products of her over-active imagination with her readers. She writes contemporary, western, and light-hearted paranormal romances. The stories are humorous yet emotional, usually with a large cast of family or friends, and a guaranteed happily-ever-after.

Vivian lives in British Columbia, Canada, with her husband of many years—her inspiration for every hero and a willing companion for all sorts of adventures.

Find out more at www.vivianarend.com.

www.ingramcontent.com/pod-product-compliance
Lightning Source LLC
Chambersburg PA
CBHW031004210726
48290CB00007B/2474